Spooky Stories

Spooky Stories

Written by
Caroline Repchuk, Claire Keene,
Geoff Cowan, Kat Wootton and Candy Wallace

Illustrated by
Diana Catchpole, Robin Edmonds,
Chris Forsey and Claire Mumford

This is a Parragon Book
This edition published in 2000

Parragon
Queen Street House,
4 Queen Street,
Bath BA1 1HE,UK

Produced by
The Templar Company plc,
Pippbrook Mill, London Road,
Dorking, Surrey RH4 1JE, UK

Edited by
Caroline Repchuk

Designed by
Caroline Reeves

Printed and bound in Italy
ISBN 0-75254-478-0(Paperback)
ISBN 0-75253-743-1(Hardback)

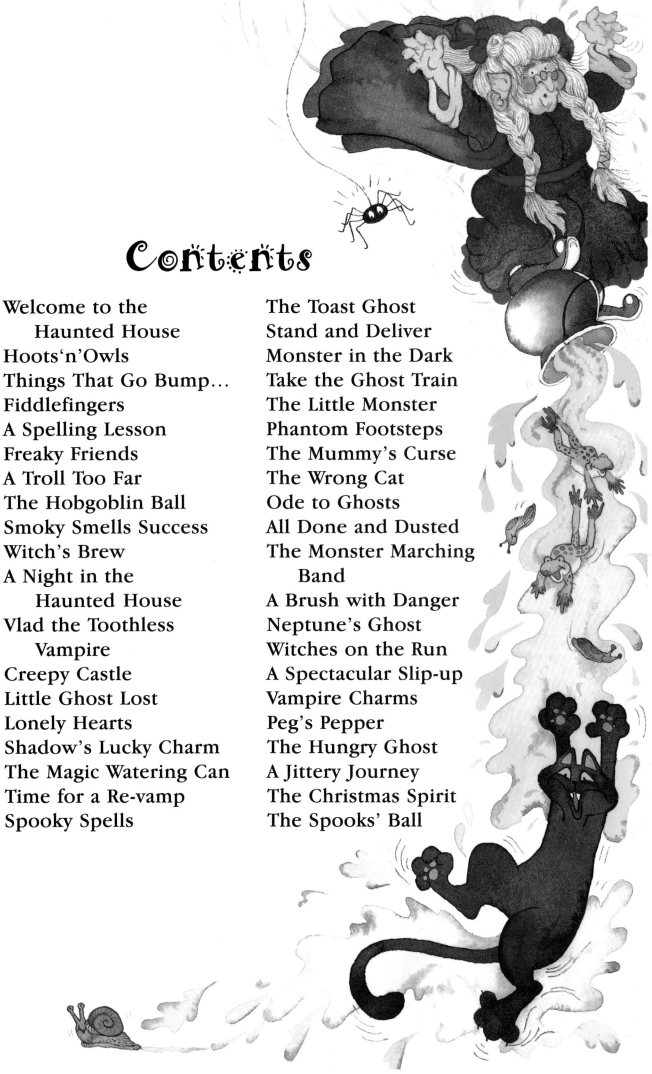

Contents

Welcome to the Haunted House!

Step in through the rusty gates —
Be quiet as a mouse.
We're going to sneak, and take
a peek, inside the Haunted House!

Ghosts are hooting in the hallway.
Ghastly ghouls lurk on the stairs.
Imps and sprites have pillow fights
to catch you unawares!

In the kitchen there's a wizard,
making slug and spider pies.
They're for a very special meal —
A Halloween surprise!

Upstairs in the dusty bedrooms
skeletons are getting dressed.
Vampires brush their hair and teeth.
All the spooks must look their best!

An empty suit of shiny armour
is clanking loudly down the hall,
to a party in the ballroom —
It's the Monster's Secret Ball!

So while the party's in full swing,
be quiet as a mouse.
Tiptoe out while you still can —
Escape the Haunted House!

Hoots 'n' Owls

"OWWW!" A horrible howl rang out through the darkness. Beneath the moon, Hairy the Horrible Hound sat staring at his paws. After a minute the ghostly dog raised his head and howled again.

Hairy had been howling away all evening. He wanted someone to talk to, someone to play with. But because he was a ghost hound no one would come near, let alone throw him a stick to chase. So he lay with his head on his shadowy paws and howled even more loudly.

The moon shone between the clouds and lit up the ruined manor house on top of the hill. The people who once lived there had fled years ago. Now it was just the haunt of three old ghosts...

Shiver, a nervous spook, was resting upstairs on a broken four-poster bed. At the first sound of Hairy's howls, he slid under the tattered sheets and pulled them tightly over his head.

Downstairs, another ghost named Grumblegroan woke with a start. As usual, he had been dozing on a crumpled old sofa.

"What the...? Doesn't Hairy the Horrible Hound ever stop howling?!" muttered Grumblegroan, miserably.

Meanwhile, Bone Idle, a skeleton, came clattering out of his favourite hiding place, a secret chamber behind the bookcase in the library.

"Pah!" he cried. "That dreadful noise goes right through my skull!"

When the howling finally stopped, all three spooks met in the hall.

"It's too much for a soul to bear!"
hissed Shiver.

"How can a ghost rest in peace around
here?!" yawned Grumblegroan.

"Something must be done about Hairy!"
wailed Bone Idle.

But what? After all, Hairy certainly sounded
like a very fierce phantom. And the three
ghosts were a lazy lot. They weren't very good
at doing anything — especially as there was
never anything to do! So, with much
muttering, sighing and moaning, the spooks
sulkily decided to do nothing at all. They
certainly weren't about to move house!
After all, Hairy's howls were the only thing
that ever disturbed them. Apart from that the
house was as silent as a grave. But suddenly,
on the landing, Shiver heard another call.

"HOO-HOOOOOOO!"

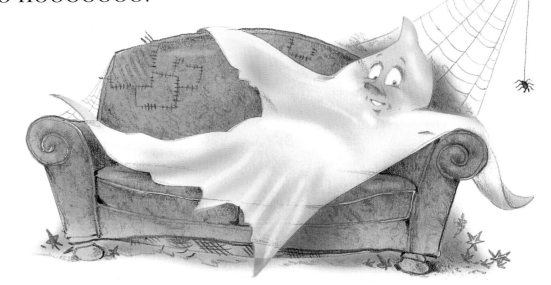

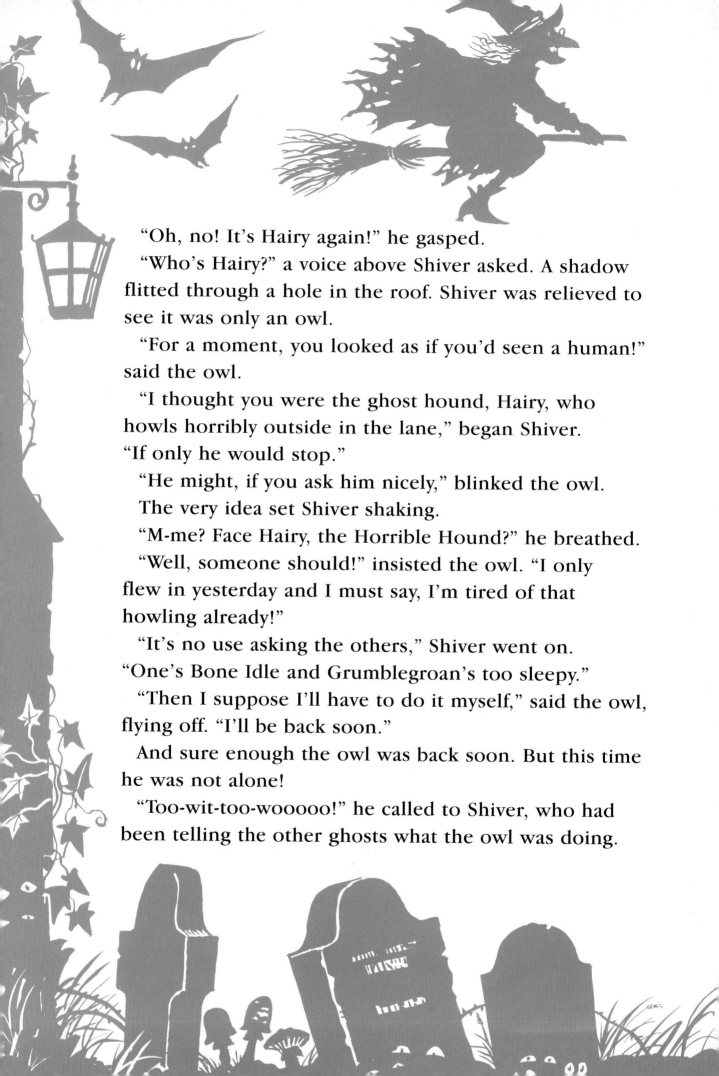

"Oh, no! It's Hairy again!" he gasped.

"Who's Hairy?" a voice above Shiver asked. A shadow flitted through a hole in the roof. Shiver was relieved to see it was only an owl.

"For a moment, you looked as if you'd seen a human!" said the owl.

"I thought you were the ghost hound, Hairy, who howls horribly outside in the lane," began Shiver. "If only he would stop."

"He might, if you ask him nicely," blinked the owl.

The very idea set Shiver shaking.

"M-me? Face Hairy, the Horrible Hound?" he breathed.

"Well, someone should!" insisted the owl. "I only flew in yesterday and I must say, I'm tired of that howling already!"

"It's no use asking the others," Shiver went on. "One's Bone Idle and Grumblegroan's too sleepy."

"Then I suppose I'll have to do it myself," said the owl, flying off. "I'll be back soon."

And sure enough the owl was back soon. But this time he was not alone!

"Too-wit-too-wooooo!" he called to Shiver, who had been telling the other ghosts what the owl was doing.

All three heard the bird hoot. Then came Hairy's dreaded howl. It was louder and closer than ever before! There was a padding of paws on the front door before it swung open on its creaky hinges.

"Yikes! Time I disappeared!" trembled Shiver. But it was too late! In swept the owl, followed by the huge, ghostly hound. Shiver clung so tightly to Bone Idle that the skeleton rattled from top to toe. For once, Grumblegroan's eyes were open wide.

"Ready for a hair-raising encounter?" joked the owl, pointing with a wing-tip to the large, ambling dog. To the three spooks' amazement, the ghost hound looked as harmless as an overgrown pup.

"Hairy told me that he only howls because he's lonely," said the owl. "He chases anything that moves, too,

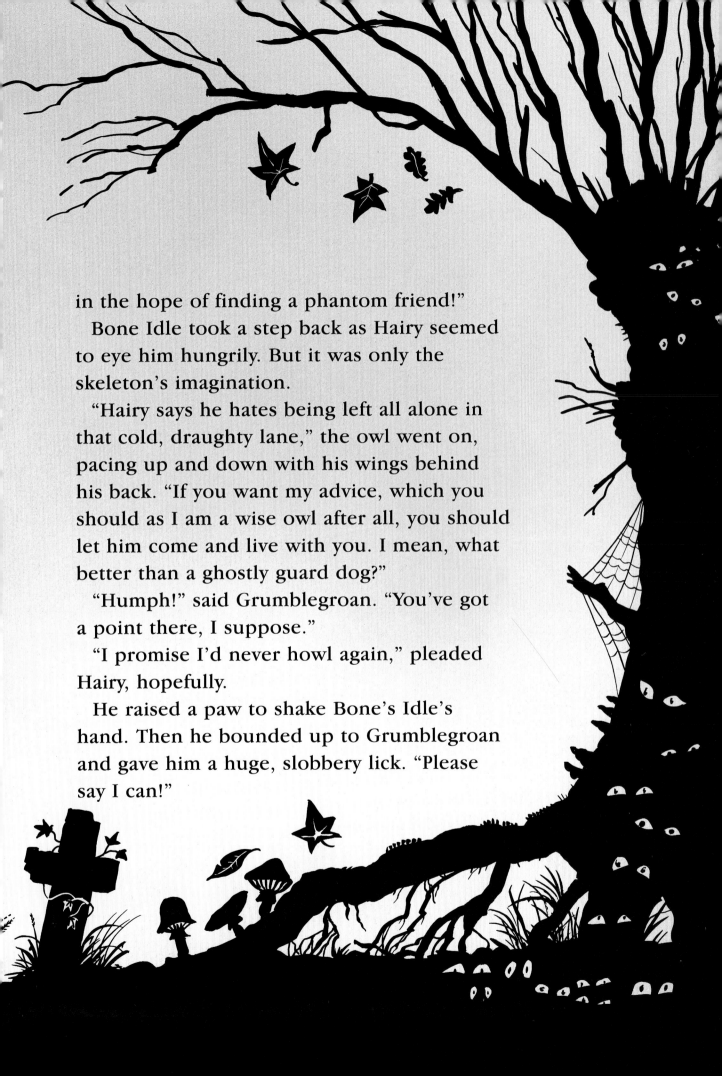

in the hope of finding a phantom friend!"

Bone Idle took a step back as Hairy seemed to eye him hungrily. But it was only the skeleton's imagination.

"Hairy says he hates being left all alone in that cold, draughty lane," the owl went on, pacing up and down with his wings behind his back. "If you want my advice, which you should as I am a wise owl after all, you should let him come and live with you. I mean, what better than a ghostly guard dog?"

"Humph!" said Grumblegroan. "You've got a point there, I suppose."

"I promise I'd never howl again," pleaded Hairy, hopefully.

He raised a paw to shake Bone's Idle's hand. Then he bounded up to Grumblegroan and gave him a huge, slobbery lick. "Please say I can!"

"Oh, very well. Anything! Just...uhh!...stop making that horrid noise!" moaned Grumblegroan.

"You can lie beside my old bed, Hairy," smiled Shiver, who wasn't the least bit nervous now.

"Great!" barked the ghost hound. "I'm so happy I could howww...."

"No, please don't!" begged Bone Idle. "You did promise. Remember?"

And so Hairy, the Horrible Hound, had found a home at last. As for the owl, he soon took flight again. But if the three ghosts had hoped for some peace and quiet, they were to be sadly disappointed. For Hairy never left them alone. If he wasn't playfully pulling the sheets off Shiver, he would leap on to Grumblegroan's lap for company.

And whenever Bone Idle tried to tiptoe away to his hidden chamber, the ghost hound thought the skeleton wanted him to play haunt and seek!

Slowly, though, the lazy spooks grew to like things being more lively. Which was just as well, or Hairy may have had to start howling again!

Things that go Bump

While you are tucked up, fast asleep,
out from dark corners
strange things creep.

But steady your nerves, don't take fright,
when things go bump in the night!

Ghosts glide down the hallway,
sneak under your bed,
and pull at the pillows
where you rest your head.

But steady your nerves, don't take fright,
when things go bump in the night!

Spooks pull off your blankets.
They tweak at your toes.
They use small white feathers
to tickle your nose.
But steady your nerves, don't take fright,
when things go bump in the night!

Ghouls empty your toybox.
They try on your clothes.
They tie up your teddy
with pink satin bows.

But steady your nerves, don't take fright,
when things go bump in the night!

The ghosts like to feast at the end of your bed.
They leave behind spilt drinks,
and stale crumbs of bread.

But steady your nerves, don't take fright,
when things go bump in the night!

For night-time's the time when
the spooks like to play.
At the first sign of daylight,
they hurry away.
So steady your nerves, don't take fright
When things go bump in the night!

Fiddlefingers

Captain Brassbuttons hummed happily and tapped his feet to a lively tune on board his pirate ship, *The Jolly Jig*. Every now and then, he would stop to stroke his bushy beard and laugh loudly while he watched some of his cut-throat crew dance a hornpipe. Around him other pirates played pipes, tambourines and accordions. The sound drifted up from below deck to a sinister skull-and-crossbones flag waving high above on the mast.

"Look lively, lads! Ha-ha-ha!" bellowed Captain Brassbuttons, who was really enjoying himself.

So were his loyal band of buccaneers. Although they were armed to the teeth with pistols and cutlasses, the weapons were now next to useless and rusting badly. You see, the pirates preferred to make music and have a merry time. After all, raiding ships and carrying off their treasure was hard and dangerous work, which was one of the reasons why they had not done it in a very long time.

But there was another reason, too. These days, *The Jolly Jig* and her crew spent most of their time at the bottom of the sea — for *The Jolly Jig* was a ghost ship and Captain Brassbuttons and his colourful crew were ghost pirates!

"'Tis a pity we don't have a fiddle player

among us, cap'n," said Patch one day,
as he rested a moment against the ship's
big, wooden wheel.

"To be sure!" sighed Brassbuttons. "That
would be more of a treasure than all the
booty we've ever bagged!"

"But that's enough fun for now, me
hearties," continued Brassbuttons, "for 'tis
high time we made ready to set sail again!"

"Aye, aye, cap'n!" said Patch and in no time
the crew were cheerfully busying themselves.
They hauled on ropes, unfurled the ghostly
white sails and made ready to raise their
phantom ship above the waves. Meanwhile,
Captain Brassbuttons hurried to his cabin to
put on his best boots, waistcoat and hat.

A short while later, *The Jolly Jig* rose
majestically from beneath the waves to haunt
the high seas, which it did whenever the
moon was full.

Passengers on passing ships would stare in amazement at the sight of the fantastic phantom ship. From its glowing decks came the sound of music and merry voices, as the creepy crew sang and played. What's more, the ghostly ship was thought to bring good luck to all who saw it.

But all that was about to change. That night, as the moon faded, *The Jolly Jig* sank again towards its watery grave. But, as it was about to touch the bottom, a strong under-sea current picked the ghost ship up and swept it along. Brassbuttons and his men were horrified. All they could do was hang on grimly while *The Jolly Jig* did its own wild dance along the ocean floor. At last, the ship settled and its shaken crew floated out from their hiding places.

"Shiver me timbers!" uttered Bones. "That was enough to set any ghost a-quaking and a-shaking!"

Captain Brassbuttons drifted up on to the deck to check *The Jolly Jig* was still in one piece. To his surprise, the wreck of another old vessel lay in the soft sand nearby.

"Ahoy, me hearties!" Brassbuttons called his men and pointed eagerly. "'Tis time to go a-pirating again!"

And before long the pirate raiding party set off in their longboat, rowing just above the sea-bed towards the wreck.

The battered ship lay on its side with
a huge hole in the hull. An octopus came
scuttling out. Some sharks swam past too,
eyeing the pirates coldly.

"We'd all be sharks' bait if we were flesh
and bones!" whispered Pigtail.

"Stand by to board," growled Brassbuttons,
leading his sea spooks on to the ship.

He was first to enter the crew's quarters.
There was a terrible noise coming from a
dark corner which made his knees knock
and his shoulders tremble.

"Who goes there?" he called, trying to sound
brave and fearless. Then he saw that the noise
was coming from a phantom figure lying fast
asleep in a hammock, and snoring loudly.

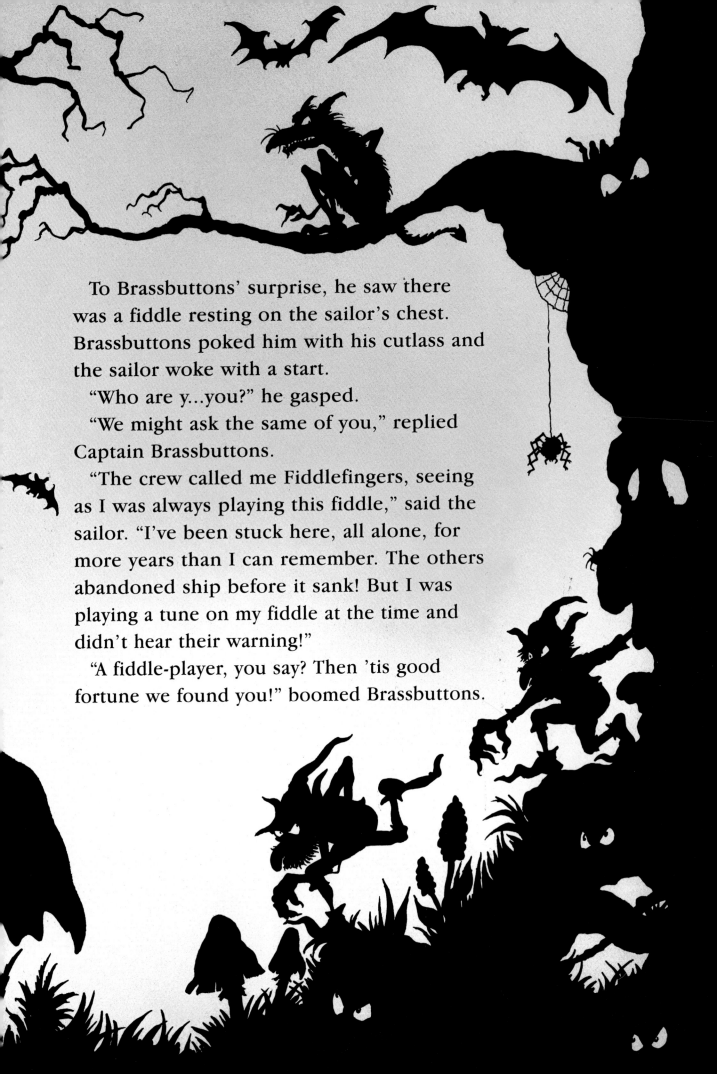

To Brassbuttons' surprise, he saw there
was a fiddle resting on the sailor's chest.
Brassbuttons poked him with his cutlass and
the sailor woke with a start.

"Who are y...you?" he gasped.

"We might ask the same of you," replied
Captain Brassbuttons.

"The crew called me Fiddlefingers, seeing
as I was always playing this fiddle," said the
sailor. "I've been stuck here, all alone, for
more years than I can remember. The others
abandoned ship before it sank! But I was
playing a tune on my fiddle at the time and
didn't hear their warning!"

"A fiddle-player, you say? Then 'tis good
fortune we found you!" boomed Brassbuttons.

However, the captain and his crew soon changed their minds. No sooner had they welcomed Fiddlefingers aboard *The Jolly Jig* than he began to play his fiddle. But what a shock for the other merry-makers. For instead of the tuneful harmony they had so been looking forward to hearing, he made a fearful, scratching screech. It was the most terrible sound the phantom pirates had ever heard. Yet, strangely, Fiddlefingers didn't seem to notice. He just went on playing happily as the other pirates winced.

"No wonder the rest of his crew fled!" grumbled Bones, his bony fingers in his ears.

But rough and ready as he seemed, Captain Brassbuttons was really a kindly soul. He felt sorry for Fiddlefingers left for so long without any ship's company and he didn't have the heart to send him on his watery way again.

So that gloomy day spelled doom for the
sorry spooks aboard *The Jolly Jig*. There was
no more laughter, dancing or merry music.
Instead, all that could be heard when the
ghost ship next appeared beneath the full
moon were the woeful wails, horrified howls
and ghastly groans of her poor suffering crew,
as they tried to drown out the sound of the
awful fiddling. As for Fiddlefingers, he just
smiled happily and played on, and on,
and on ...

A Spelling Lesson!

Wanda Witch went wandering,
Within a spooky wood.
She loved to practise spooky spells,
And hated being good!

Wanda turned some bluebells,
Into smelly, slimy goo.
She gave a tree a creepy face,
To scare the likes of you!

She crept up on a wizard,
And before he could respond,
Wanda waved her wand and he
Fell straight into a pond!

Although it was not very deep,
The wizard soon saw red.
He cast a spell which made his cloak,
Flap right round Wanda's head.

It wrapped around her body,
And squeezed her really tight.
"Say sorry," roared the wizard,
"Or stay like that all night!"

The witch agreed and told him,
"Your magic is so fast.
No more naughty spells from me,
I've really cast my last!"

Freaky Friends

Having an old witch as her next-door-neighbour was the last thing that Victoria Vampire wanted. No sooner had Winnie moved in, complete with her broomstick, cauldron, pointed hat and all manner of pots and potions, than weird things began to happen.

Whenever Winnie stirred up a magical brew indoors, a mass of stars and sparks would fly out of the chimney of her tumbledown old cottage like a fantastic firework show.

They whizzed safely beyond her own little cottage garden — and landed in the grounds of Victoria's dark and spooky house instead! Victoria's clean washing was soon spotted with sooty marks and two big holes were burned in her best black cloak.

Then there was the smell, or more precisely, the stinky pong! Whatever was bubbling away in Winnie's cauldron, it was definitely *not* leek and potato soup. The awful aroma wafted across into the dark turrets of Victoria's home. In no time it had disturbed Victoria's precious colony of bats that lived in the attic. They poured like black treacle out of a small skylight and fluttered away to hide in a dark, distant cave. And as if losing her pets wasn't bad enough, Victoria had to keep every door and window tightly closed against the stink. It was enough to make her flash her fangs in anger!

But there was worse to come. Winnie's two cats, Scratch and Sniff, were mouse-mad, they chased them non-stop. So one day, when they spotted some by Victoria's woodshed, the mean-eyed cats set off in hot pursuit. The trouble was that Victoria had just entered the shed to fetch some logs for her fire. Now, being a vampire, she didn't like going out in daylight and, as usual, was wearing her dark sunglasses. So she didn't see Scratch and Sniff slink into the shed — she just felt the sting of their claws as she tripped over them and they lashed out at her legs. Victoria let out a blood-curdling scream, the startled cats screeched 'YEOWWL!', wood went flying and so did Victoria! She crashed into the door, bumping her head and breaking an arm off her precious sunglasses.

Meanwhile, the cats sulkily slipped away, having lost the mice who had taken advantage of all the commotion and disappeared.

Victoria tried to balance her broken sunglasses back on her nose. Then she felt inside her mouth and winced — she had broken one of her fine fangs when she fell over. That was the last straw!

"That does it!" she hissed. "I'm going to have a not-so-neighbourly word with that pesky witch!"

Victoria marched straight out of her own gate, up the front path to Winnie's cottage and thumped on the door. But Winnie was in the back garden, practising some spelling. She was concentrating so hard that she did not hear the visiting vampire. Winnie waved her wand at a carpet-beater lying on the lawn. Nearby, a large, dusty rug hung on the washing line.

"Eye of newt and lizard's spleen, carpet-beater start to *clean!*" she chanted.

"There you are!" cried Victoria, stomping around the side of the cottage. "I've got a bone to pick with you."

"Oh, good. Come inside, then. I'm hungry, too," said Winnie, smiling innocently at her.

Victoria was about to set Winnie straight and give her a piece of her mind, when she suddenly stopped dead in her tracks. Something was floating towards her.

It was the carpet-beater. Instead of giving the rug a good dusting, it swished and swiped at Victoria.

"Ooh! Aagh! Help!" she wailed as the carpet beater chased her out of Winnie's garden and all the way home. There she sat and sulked until the moon rose.

"Enough's enough!" she thought. "It's time I taught that tiresome witch a lesson!" She stomped out into the darkness, and was soon hard at work in Winnie's garden, pulling up all the magic plants and trampling on the special herb patch. Then she spied Scratch and Sniff curled up fast asleep in a basket by an open window. Reaching in with both hands she caught hold of their long whiskers and pulled with all her might — Ping! Ping! Ping! The furious cats howled in pain and leapt in the air. But, using some special

vampire magic of her own, Victoria turned herself into a bat and took off into the night. But she hadn't flown far when, suddenly, something whizzed past her like a rocket. It was Winnie on her broomstick.

Caught in its slipstream, Victoria was tossed about like a leaf in a storm. She had just made a bumpy landing on Winnie's lawn when the witch swooped down and landed right on top of her! As Scratch prepared to pounce, thinking bat might make a tasty alternative to mouse, Victoria changed back with a flash. But she was bruised and breathless.

"Ohh! My back!" Victoria groaned.

"Deary me!" wailed the witch. "It's all my fault! I had no idea it was you! Here, please let me help!"

Victoria was too weary to argue. And help Winnie certainly did.

Over the next few days, nothing was too much trouble for her. She insisted that Victoria rest at home in bed while she cooked a surprisingly tasty beetroot soup. It was such a deliciously deep red colour that Victoria had to have some.

"It would have been better if those pesky cats hadn't dug up my herbs, mind you," said Winnie. While Victoria guiltily enjoyed another bowlful, Winnie searched her spell book

"Aha! I knew it was here somewhere!" she said. Winnie waved her wand and chanted something about taking care of canines. Then, in a flash, Victoria's two beautiful, long sharp teeth were perfect again.

"*Fangs* very much," she joked.

Further spells repaired the holes in
Victoria's cloak, cleaned up her washing,
and brought her bats back to the loft.
Another spell made Winnie's broom sweep up
the wood-shed. Scratch and Sniff eagerly
caught every mouse in Victoria's house (which
made up a bit for losing their whiskers!).
Victoria felt ashamed for trying to teach the
kind witch a lesson.

"I feel so much better," smiled Victoria,
getting up at last. "You're a wonder, Winnie!"

"Nonsense! Nothing like a *spell* in bed,"
the witch replied, modestly, as she gave her
new-found friend a hug.

A Troll too Far

Once upon a time, in a faraway fairytale
kingdom, there lived a king with a problem
— a very big, very nasty problem indeed.
Now, the king lived in a proper fairytale
castle, with towers and turrets, ballrooms and
battlements, a wide, deep moat and a drawbridge.
And underneath that drawbridge lived and lurked
a very large, very smelly, very HUNGRY troll!

Beware
of the
TROLL

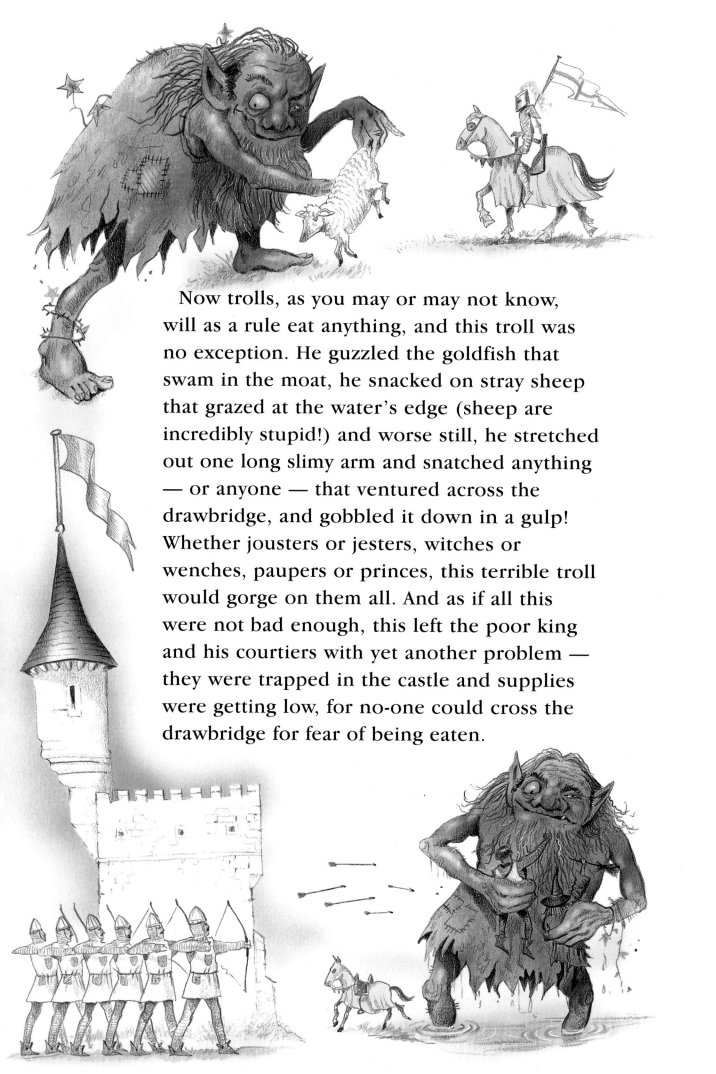

Now trolls, as you may or may not know, will as a rule eat anything, and this troll was no exception. He guzzled the goldfish that swam in the moat, he snacked on stray sheep that grazed at the water's edge (sheep are incredibly stupid!) and worse still, he stretched out one long slimy arm and snatched anything — or anyone — that ventured across the drawbridge, and gobbled it down in a gulp! Whether jousters or jesters, witches or wenches, paupers or princes, this terrible troll would gorge on them all. And as if all this were not bad enough, this left the poor king and his courtiers with yet another problem — they were trapped in the castle and supplies were getting low, for no-one could cross the drawbridge for fear of being eaten.

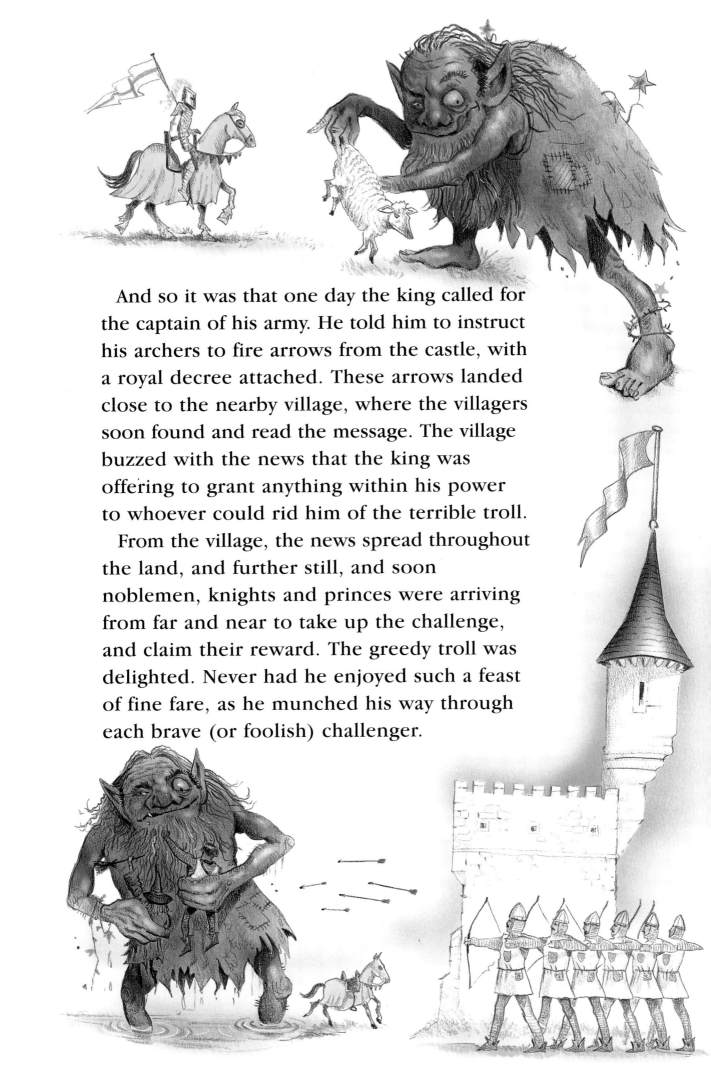

And so it was that one day the king called for the captain of his army. He told him to instruct his archers to fire arrows from the castle, with a royal decree attached. These arrows landed close to the nearby village, where the villagers soon found and read the message. The village buzzed with the news that the king was offering to grant anything within his power to whoever could rid him of the terrible troll.

From the village, the news spread throughout the land, and further still, and soon noblemen, knights and princes were arriving from far and near to take up the challenge, and claim their reward. The greedy troll was delighted. Never had he enjoyed such a feast of fine fare, as he munched his way through each brave (or foolish) challenger.

The king was in despair. Could no one save them from their castle prison? Then, just as he had almost given up hope, a lumbering shape came looming through the mist.

"*I* will rid you of this terrible troll," boomed a deep and dreadful voice. As the mist cleared the king saw to his horror that the voice belonged to an even larger, even uglier, even smellier troll! But what could the king do? He was certainly not about to argue!

And so the new troll leapt into the moat and a fearsome fight took place. The two trolls thrashed and splashed, bit and scratched, pulled and tugged, roared and gnashed their teeth. They sent tidal waves crashing around the moat, and shook the castle to its foundations!

Finally, after three days and nights of monstrous struggling, the old troll was forced to accept defeat, and he stomped away into the distance, cursing and shaking his fist.

"And now for my reward!" smirked the new troll, with a gleam in his eye, slowly licking his lips. The king shuddered, and clasped the princesses tightly to him. Anything but his precious daughters!

"What is your request," stuttered the king. "I will grant you anything in my power, as I promised."

"I'd like a new home," drawled the troll. "Beneath the drawbridge..."

"Open wide," called young Princess Grace. From beneath the drawbridge, the hideous head of the revolting new troll appeared, mouth open wide to reveal a rotting row of yellow teeth.

"Yum, yum, breakfast!" slobbered the troll. The princess leaned over the drawbridge and poured a vast vat of cakes and cabbages into the troll's quivering, dribbling, open mouth.

For yes, he was huge, he was smelly, he was hideous. But he was also *vegetarian* — and the king was delighted!

The Hobgoblin Ball

Late at night when the moon is bright,
　And the air is soft and still,
　Pixies peep and fairies creep,
And goblins roam at will.

Through the trees, a gentle breeze
Stirs brownies from their dreams.
Imps awake, they stretch and shake,
Then slide along moonbeams.

Elves sneak out, and slink about,
Leprechauns come leaping.
Little sprites wave magic lights,
While the world is sleeping.

Singing songs, they skip along,
Towards the forest glade.
Hung with lights, all twinkling bright,
While gentle music's played.

They appear, from far and near,
A host of fairy folk.
This happy band dance hand in hand,
Beneath the magic oak.

Every night, enchanting sights
Await for one and all.
So when day's done, come join the fun,
At the great Hobgoblin Ball!

Smoky Smells Success

Smoky was a spook, and a very happy spook at that! He haunted an ancient castle, surrounded by a wide moat. From deep in its darkest dungeons to high on the heights of its battlements, Smoky would appear, mischievously and mysteriously, whenever he wanted. Sometimes, he appeared just as himself — a swirling puff of supernatural smoke. However, being a ghost, Smoky could change shape at will.

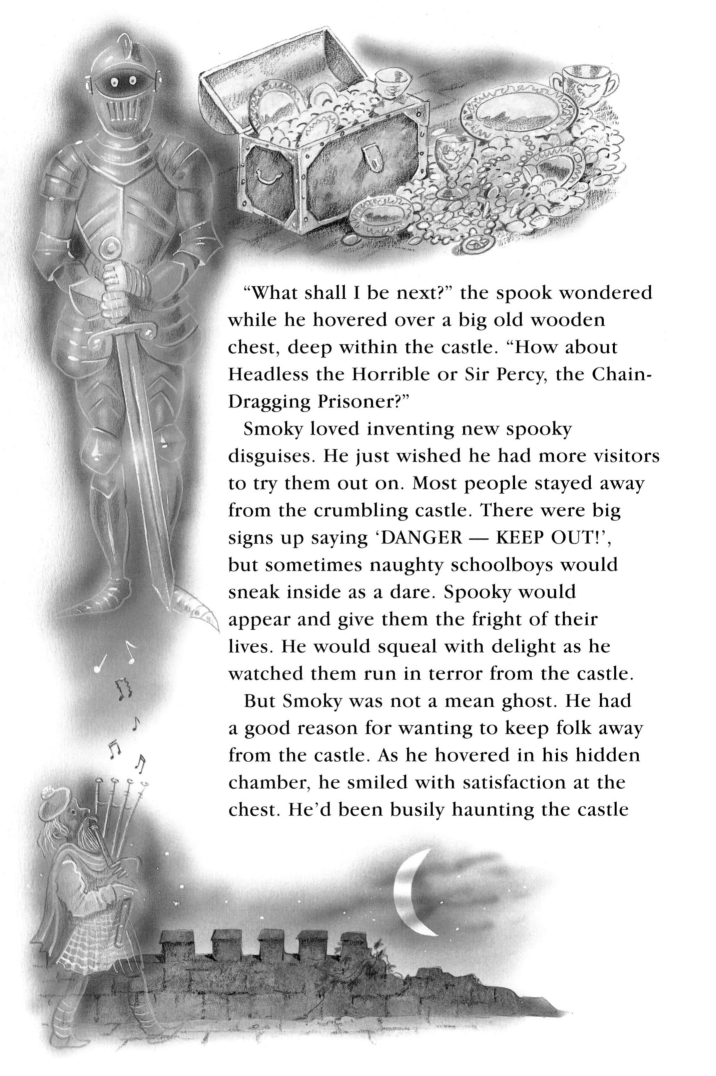

"What shall I be next?" the spook wondered while he hovered over a big old wooden chest, deep within the castle. "How about Headless the Horrible or Sir Percy, the Chain-Dragging Prisoner?"

Smoky loved inventing new spooky disguises. He just wished he had more visitors to try them out on. Most people stayed away from the crumbling castle. There were big signs up saying 'DANGER — KEEP OUT!', but sometimes naughty schoolboys would sneak inside as a dare. Spooky would appear and give them the fright of their lives. He would squeal with delight as he watched them run in terror from the castle.

But Smoky was not a mean ghost. He had a good reason for wanting to keep folk away from the castle. As he hovered in his hidden chamber, he smiled with satisfaction at the chest. He'd been busily haunting the castle

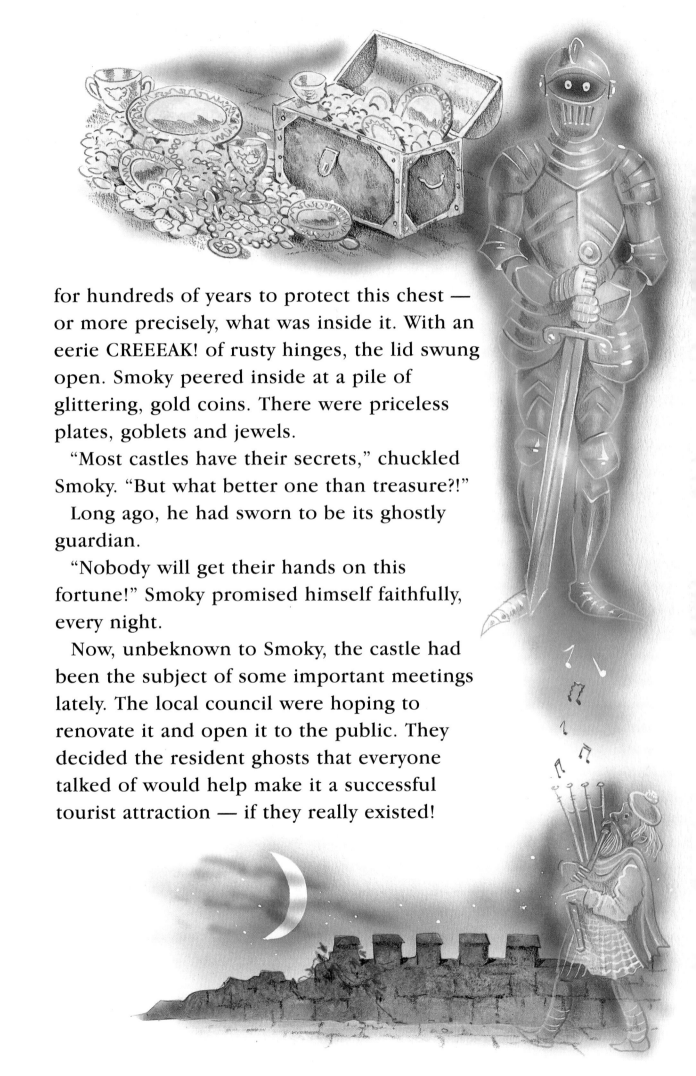

for hundreds of years to protect this chest — or more precisely, what was inside it. With an eerie CREEEAK! of rusty hinges, the lid swung open. Smoky peered inside at a pile of glittering, gold coins. There were priceless plates, goblets and jewels.

"Most castles have their secrets," chuckled Smoky. "But what better one than treasure?!"

Long ago, he had sworn to be its ghostly guardian.

"Nobody will get their hands on this fortune!" Smoky promised himself faithfully, every night.

Now, unbeknown to Smoky, the castle had been the subject of some important meetings lately. The local council were hoping to renovate it and open it to the public. They decided the resident ghosts that everyone talked of would help make it a successful tourist attraction — if they really existed!

So it was that one morning, Smoky heard a car pull up. A man and woman climbed out. They walked slowly around the castle walls, making notes, and looking very serious indeed.

"It's no use," said the man. "This castle's crumbling. If we don't pull it down, it will fall all on its own. We're going to have to forget about opening it to the public."

"Pity," replied the woman. "It's such a grand, historical building. If only we could raise enough money to have it repaired. But that would cost a fortune!"

Smoky froze. For the first time, he understood what it was like to be scared! If his precious castle was pulled down, what would happen to him? He wouldn't want to haunt anywhere else. Something had to be done — and fast!

As the visitors were returning to their car, they suddenly stopped and sniffed the air. There was a wonderful smell coming from the castle. The man pointed to what looked like a thin trail of steam floating by the entrance. It was Smoky, who had conjured up a delicious smell to tempt the visitors in.

"Let's take a look inside," said the man.

"But it's dangerous — and apparently haunted!" said the woman, nervously.

"We'll be careful," said the man. "I have to find out where that incredible smell is coming from."

They followed the lovely smell into the castle. Smoky led the way, disguised as a thin trail of smoke. For once, he didn't want to frighten his visitors away! They crept quietly along the corridors, glancing nervously over their shoulders, but there were no spooks to be seen. Smoky made a secret door in one of the walls swing wide open. A narrow, cobweb-filled passage led the visitors to his hidden chamber and...the treasure chest!

When the officials saw its glittering, golden contents, they shrieked so loudly it made Smoky jump.

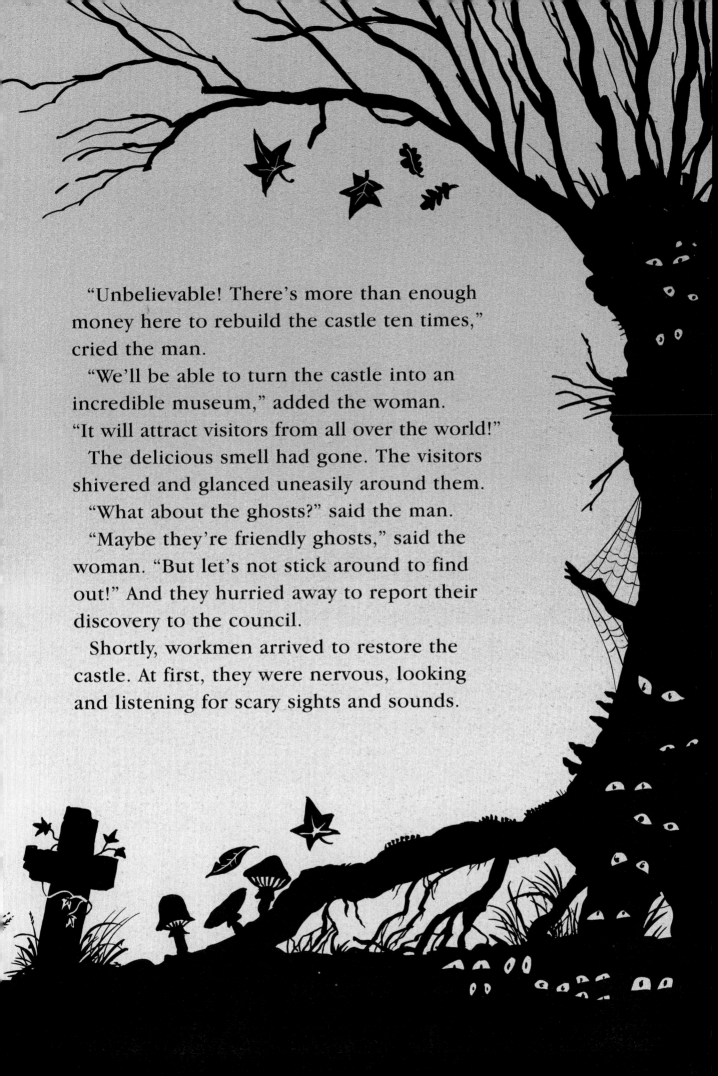

"Unbelievable! There's more than enough money here to rebuild the castle ten times," cried the man.

"We'll be able to turn the castle into an incredible museum," added the woman. "It will attract visitors from all over the world!"

The delicious smell had gone. The visitors shivered and glanced uneasily around them.

"What about the ghosts?" said the man.

"Maybe they're friendly ghosts," said the woman. "But let's not stick around to find out!" And they hurried away to report their discovery to the council.

Shortly, workmen arrived to restore the castle. At first, they were nervous, looking and listening for scary sights and sounds.

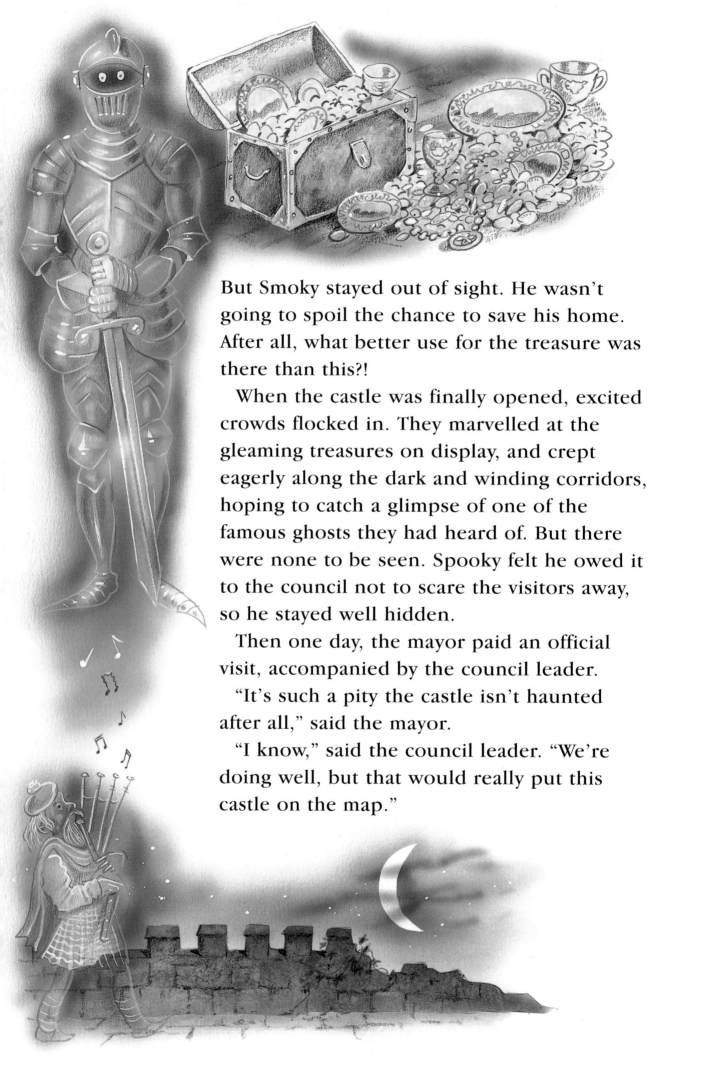

But Smoky stayed out of sight. He wasn't going to spoil the chance to save his home. After all, what better use for the treasure was there than this?!

When the castle was finally opened, excited crowds flocked in. They marvelled at the gleaming treasures on display, and crept eagerly along the dark and winding corridors, hoping to catch a glimpse of one of the famous ghosts they had heard of. But there were none to be seen. Spooky felt he owed it to the council not to scare the visitors away, so he stayed well hidden.

Then one day, the mayor paid an official visit, accompanied by the council leader.

"It's such a pity the castle isn't haunted after all," said the mayor.

"I know," said the council leader. "We're doing well, but that would really put this castle on the map."

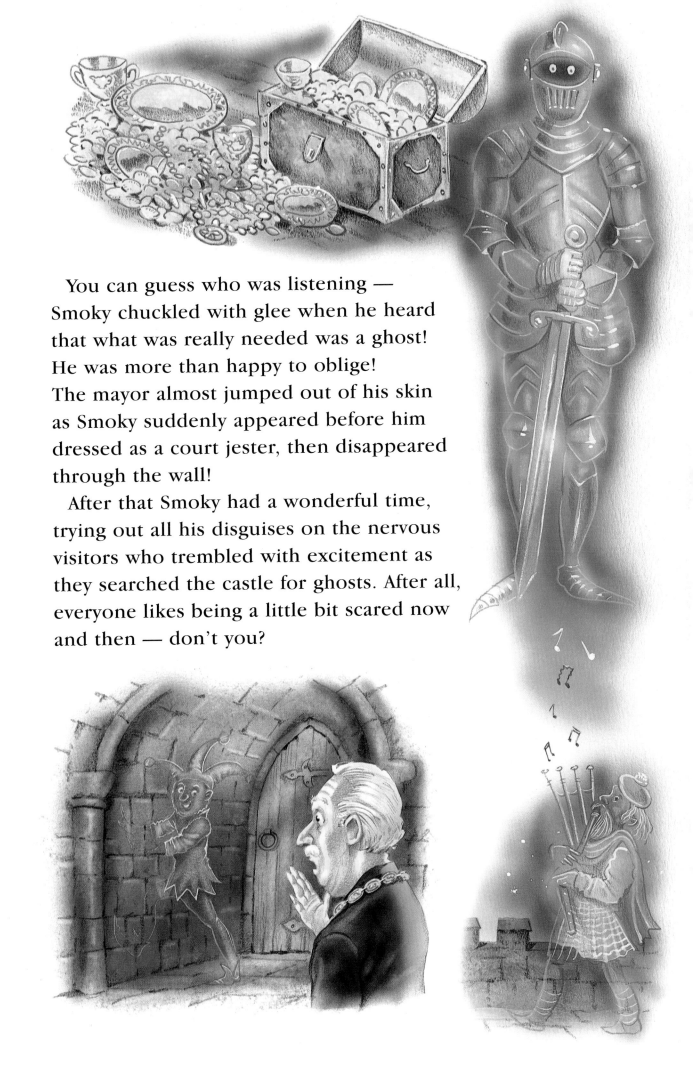

You can guess who was listening —
Smoky chuckled with glee when he heard
that what was really needed was a ghost!
He was more than happy to oblige!
The mayor almost jumped out of his skin
as Smoky suddenly appeared before him
dressed as a court jester, then disappeared
through the wall!

After that Smoky had a wonderful time,
trying out all his disguises on the nervous
visitors who trembled with excitement as
they searched the castle for ghosts. After all,
everyone likes being a little bit scared now
and then — don't you?

Witch's Brew

Eye of lizard, toe of frog,
　　Tail of rat and bark of dog.
　　Sneeze of chicken, cough of bat,
Lick of weasel, smell of cat.

Stir it up and mix it well,
To make a magic monster spell.

Leeches liver, finely chopped,
Pus of pimple, freshly popped.
Web of spider, slime of toad,
Squish of hedgehog, scraped from road.

Stir it up and mix it well,
To make a magic monster spell.

Spell for
Magic
Monster
· will help with
household chores
· will be gentle
and polite
· will definitely
not eat you

Ingredients
Eye of lizard
Toe of frog
Tail of rat
Bark of dog
Sneeze of
chicken
Cough of bat
Lick of weasel
Smell of cat

Now it's done, the spell is ready,
The monster's rising, slow and steady.
"Pleased to meet you," Witchy sighs.
"Pleased to *eat* you," he replies.

What's gone wrong, she cannot tell,
To spoil the magic monster spell.

The witch goes pale, she must act fast,
Or else this day may be her last!
She grabs her wand. She has a notion
Of how to get rid of this potion.

She shakes her wand, which breaks the spell,
And waves the monster fond farewell!

A Night in the Haunted House

High up on a lonely hill, surrounded
by a great dark forest, stood an
ancient, crumbling manor, known
as the *Haunted House*. It belonged to a
greedy old man, who everyone said was a
wizard. He lived in a little cottage in the
grounds of the manor, with just his black
cat for company. He had no friends to
speak of, but he was very happy, because
he had a true love. Now, his true love was
gold, and he had plenty of it, for he had
found a way to make the *Haunted House*
serve him well, even though he dare not
set one foot inside it himself.

He had pinned a notice to the tall rusting gates of the manor, promising a reward of five hundred gold coins to anyone who could spend a whole night inside it, and charging them five gold coins for the privilege of trying.

Desperate men and brave adventurers came from far and wide, each certain they could withstand the horrors of the *Haunted House*. Some did well, and lasted many hours before fleeing in terror. Back in the safety of the local village inn, they would mutter and gibber and stutter out tales of ghosts so ghoulish, and monsters so terrifying, that their wide-eyed listeners would gasp with horror and congratulate them for staying in the house so long. Others lasted mere minutes before fleeing into the night in shame.

Now one day, there came a man called Titan, whose bravery was legendary. He was known far and wide as the most fearless adventurer, with towering strength and nerves of steel. He paid his five gold coins to the wizard, who rather reluctantly gave him the key to the house. This fellow looked a bit too fearless for the wizard's liking.

That night, Titan stepped through the rusty gates, and strode towards the *Haunted House*. Without hesitating, he unlocked the door and went in. A butler appeared from nowhere, carrying his head under his arm. "Jeeves at your service, sir," he said, creepily. "Follow me."

"Thank you, my good man," said Titan, handing him his coat and following him up the creaking staircase without blinking an eye.

Ancient portraits followed him with their eyes. Titan winked at them as he passed. An empty suit of armour waved. Titan waved back. "Good evening," he said.

Jeeves led him on down a murky passage. A heavy door creaked open and they entered a dark bedroom, with a tattered four-poster bed. Cobwebs hung from the ceiling, and a thick layer of dust covered the furniture. Titan opened the wardrobe and a skeleton came leering out. "Oops, sorry to disturb you," Titan said, brushing the cobwebs from a chair.

The startled butler looked at Titan in amazement. Was this man scared of anything?. "Tea, sir?" Jeeves asked. "Herman will bring it up right away."

Moments later Herman, a dribbling two-headed ogre, appeared with Titan's tea. "Thank you," said Titan, pouring the tea without flinching. "That will be all."

And so it went on through the night. The inhabitants of the *Haunted House* did their worst. Ghouls wailed and werewolves howled. Mummies rose up from their tombs and staggered through the room. A ghostly prisoner appeared dragging clanking chains and vanished through the wall. Vampires leered and phantoms jeered.

"This is quite a show!" said Titan, settling back on his pillows, and watching the ghostly goings-on with a cheerful grin.

Meanwhile, down in the little cottage, the wizard kept glancing nervously at the clock, as he shone and polished his precious gold. Slowly the hours passed, and still there was no sign of Titan. Could this be the man who would finally claim the reward?

Back at the house, a fluffy white ghost was hovering over Titan's head, shouting "Boo!" and trying to sound frightening. It was his first night on the job. The startled spooks had had to call out all reserves — how were they going to frighten this man of steel?

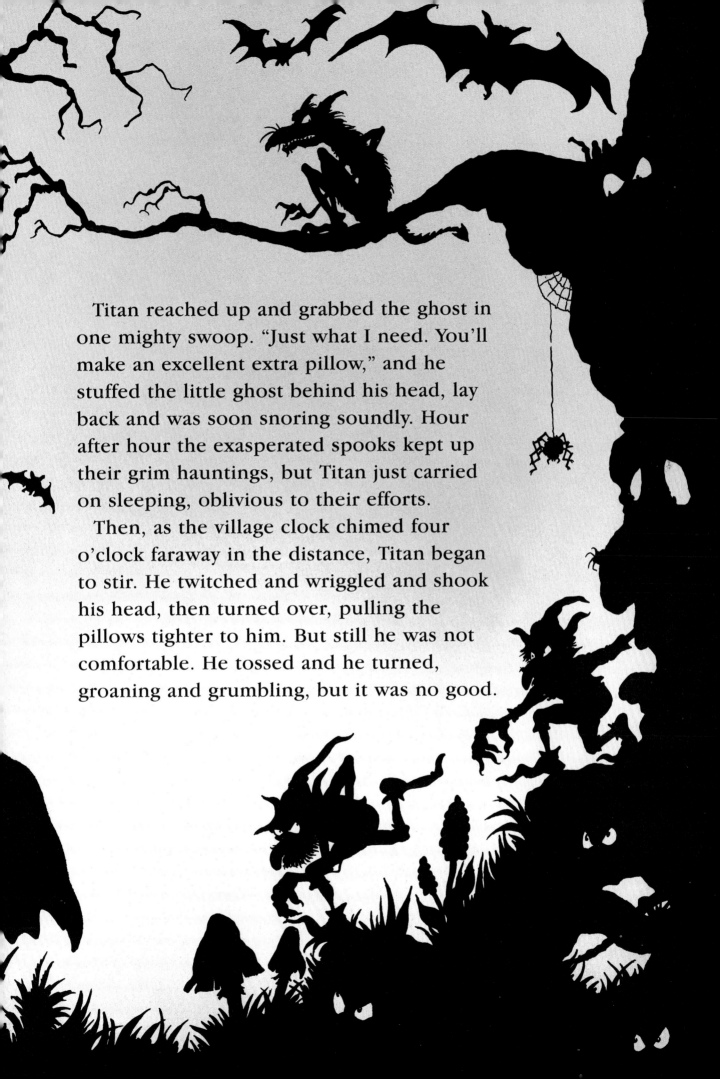

Titan reached up and grabbed the ghost in one mighty swoop. "Just what I need. You'll make an excellent extra pillow," and he stuffed the little ghost behind his head, lay back and was soon snoring soundly. Hour after hour the exasperated spooks kept up their grim hauntings, but Titan just carried on sleeping, oblivious to their efforts.

Then, as the village clock chimed four o'clock faraway in the distance, Titan began to stir. He twitched and wriggled and shook his head, then turned over, pulling the pillows tighter to him. But still he was not comfortable. He tossed and he turned, groaning and grumbling, but it was no good.

There was something lumpy underneath his pillow that was keeping him from settling back to sleep. He opened his eyes. The exhausted ghouls surged forward, renewing their efforts to terrify him.

"Oh, are you chaps still up?!" said Titan, surprised. "Don't you have beds to go to?" The weary ghosts shook their heads in exasperation. Titan felt about under his pillow. What was it that was lodged under there, keeping him awake? Just then, his hand wrapped around something small and soft and furry. He felt a shiver run down his spine. Slowly he pulled out his hand from under the pillow and there, trembling in fright was a tiny little white mouse. Titan let out an almighty scream! He leapt from the bed and raced for the door.

Down he fled through dusty passages and darkened stairways, then disappeared, still screaming and hollering, into the night.

Through his window, the wizard cackled in delight as he watched him fleeing. He hugged his bag of gold to him, and rubbed his hands together with glee.

"I knew he'd crack," he chuckled. "Something gets to all of them in the end!"

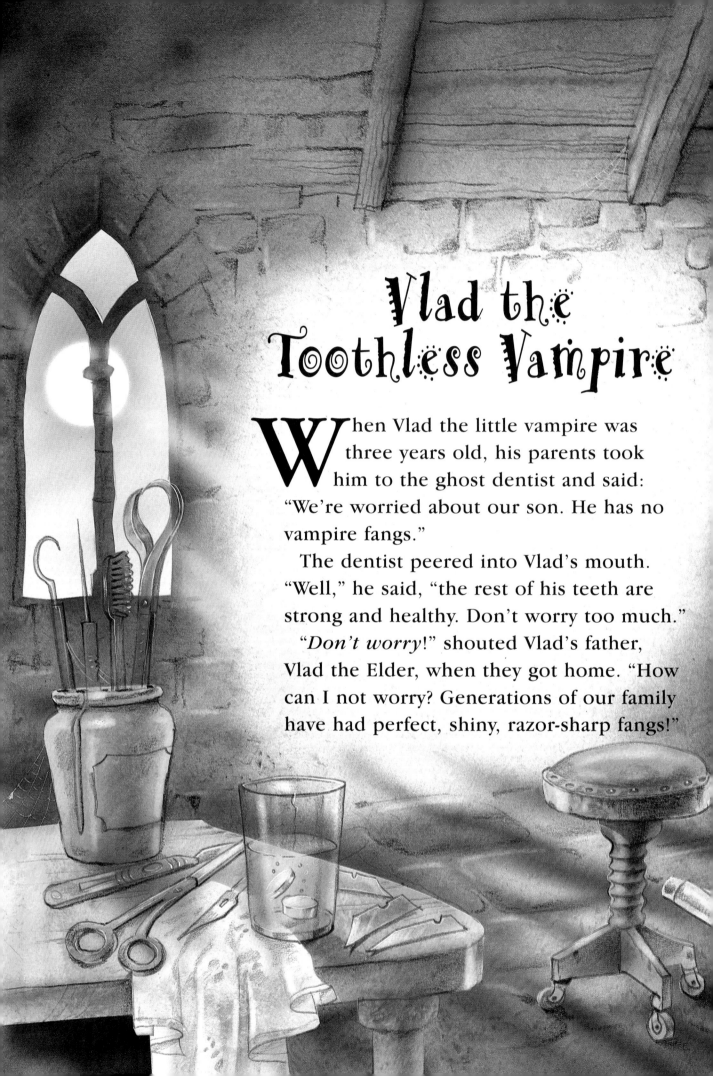

Vlad the Toothless Vampire

When Vlad the little vampire was three years old, his parents took him to the ghost dentist and said: "We're worried about our son. He has no vampire fangs."

The dentist peered into Vlad's mouth. "Well," he said, "the rest of his teeth are strong and healthy. Don't worry too much."

"*Don't worry*!" shouted Vlad's father, Vlad the Elder, when they got home. "How can I not worry? Generations of our family have had perfect, shiny, razor-sharp fangs!"

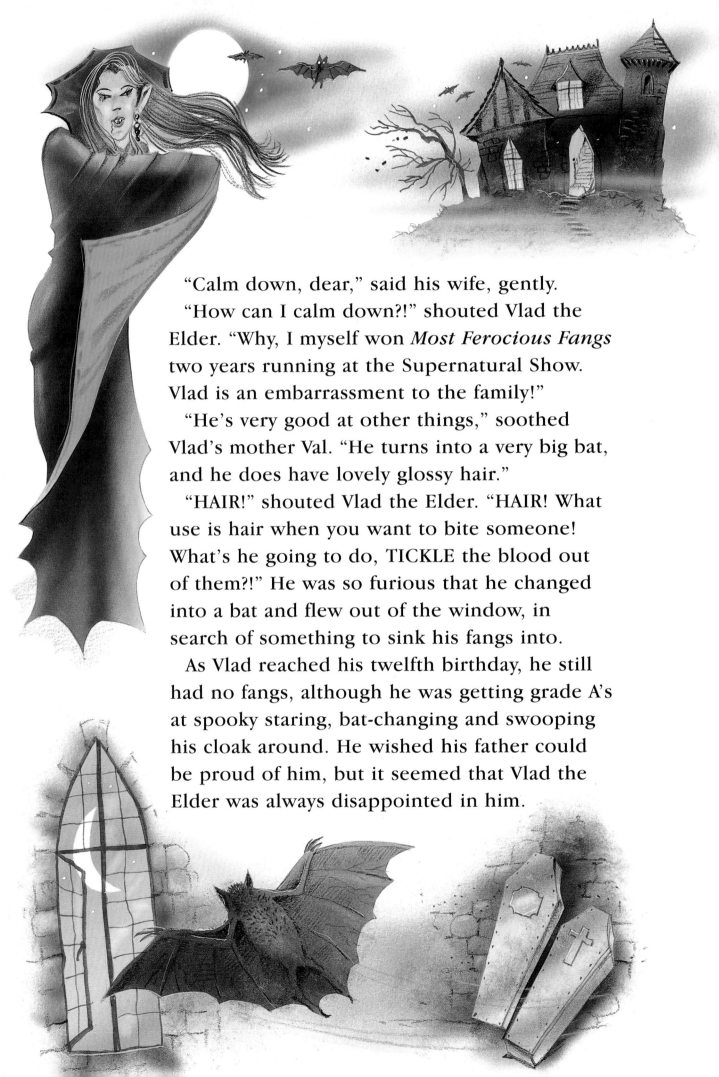

"Calm down, dear," said his wife, gently.

"How can I calm down?!" shouted Vlad the Elder. "Why, I myself won *Most Ferocious Fangs* two years running at the Supernatural Show. Vlad is an embarrassment to the family!"

"He's very good at other things," soothed Vlad's mother Val. "He turns into a very big bat, and he does have lovely glossy hair."

"HAIR!" shouted Vlad the Elder. "HAIR! What use is hair when you want to bite someone! What's he going to do, TICKLE the blood out of them?!" He was so furious that he changed into a bat and flew out of the window, in search of something to sink his fangs into.

As Vlad reached his twelfth birthday, he still had no fangs, although he was getting grade A's at spooky staring, bat-changing and swooping his cloak around. He wished his father could be proud of him, but it seemed that Vlad the Elder was always disappointed in him.

"Twelve years old and no vampire teeth!" he raged. "He'll never make a proper vampire. He's no use, no use at all!"

Young Vlad was hurt and angry: "I don't *have* to bite things!" he cried. "I could be a doctor, or a vet, or an actor!"

"Pah!" snorted his father. "A vet who only visits his patients at night? Don't be a fool, son." And he swept his cloak around his shoulders before disappearing into the night.

A short time later, a local amateur dramatic group decided to use the old abandoned house in which Vlad and his family lived as a venue for their next show.

"It's got just the right spooky atmosphere," said Brian the director, unaware the cellars housed a family of vampires, one of whom was listening to his conversation. Vlad, hanging on the lampshade disguised as a bat, looked at the script on the table. 'Dracula' it said on the cover.

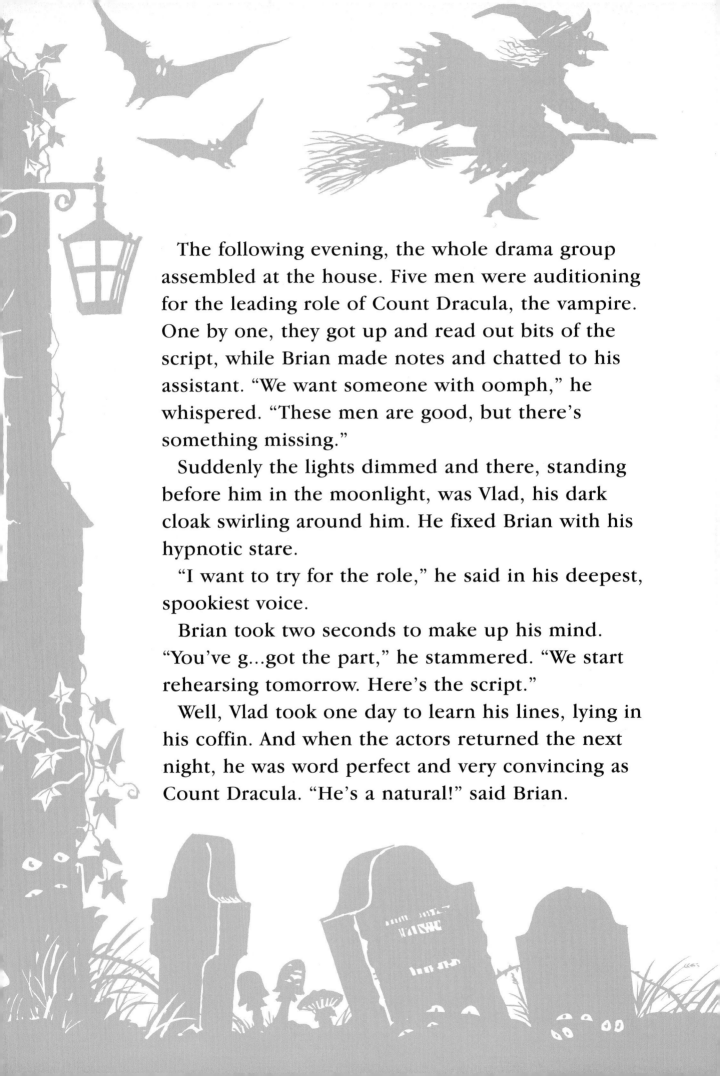

The following evening, the whole drama group assembled at the house. Five men were auditioning for the leading role of Count Dracula, the vampire. One by one, they got up and read out bits of the script, while Brian made notes and chatted to his assistant. "We want someone with oomph," he whispered. "These men are good, but there's something missing."

Suddenly the lights dimmed and there, standing before him in the moonlight, was Vlad, his dark cloak swirling around him. He fixed Brian with his hypnotic stare.

"I want to try for the role," he said in his deepest, spookiest voice.

Brian took two seconds to make up his mind. "You've g...got the part," he stammered. "We start rehearsing tomorrow. Here's the script."

Well, Vlad took one day to learn his lines, lying in his coffin. And when the actors returned the next night, he was word perfect and very convincing as Count Dracula. "He's a natural!" said Brian.

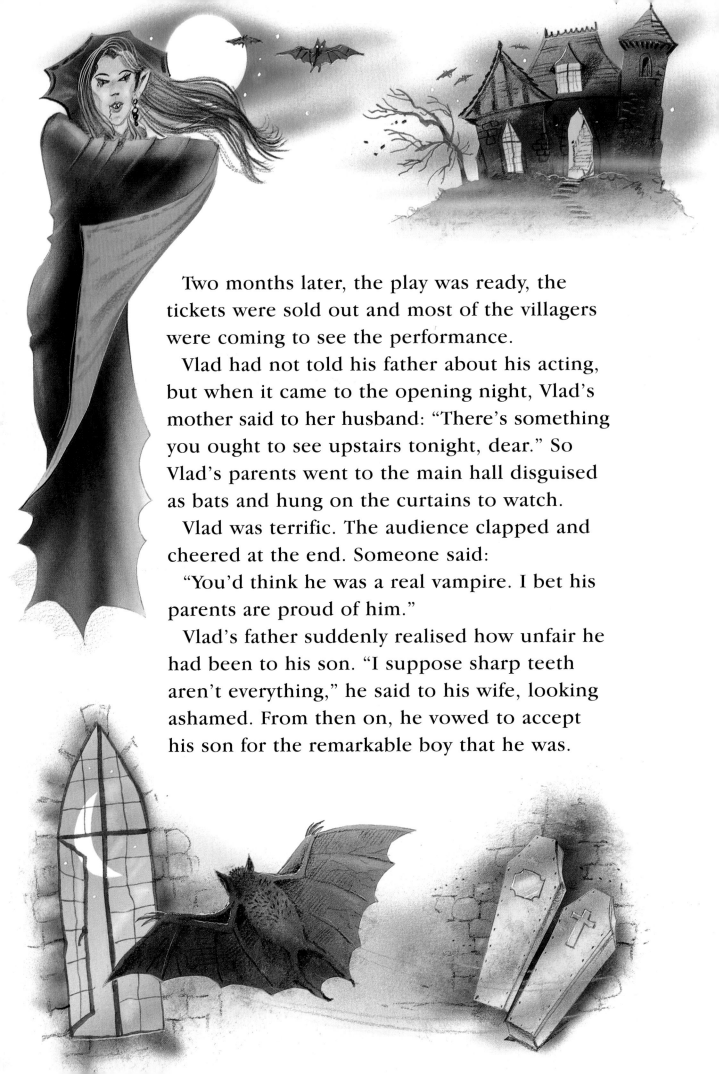

Two months later, the play was ready, the tickets were sold out and most of the villagers were coming to see the performance.

Vlad had not told his father about his acting, but when it came to the opening night, Vlad's mother said to her husband: "There's something you ought to see upstairs tonight, dear." So Vlad's parents went to the main hall disguised as bats and hung on the curtains to watch.

Vlad was terrific. The audience clapped and cheered at the end. Someone said:

"You'd think he was a real vampire. I bet his parents are proud of him."

Vlad's father suddenly realised how unfair he had been to his son. "I suppose sharp teeth aren't everything," he said to his wife, looking ashamed. From then on, he vowed to accept his son for the remarkable boy that he was.

But the next day, the young vampire woke up feeling different. There was an odd tingling in his mouth. He felt round his gums with his fingers. "Ouch!" Sure enough, poking out of his gums were two, white, shiny points.

"Yippee!" he yelled. "My vampire teeth! I fancy a BITE for breakfast!"

"Not till you've read this review of your play, son," said his father holding up the newspaper proudly. "After all, you seem to have made your mark already!"

Creepy Castle

In a castle, dark and dusty,
Stood an armour suit all rusty.
Haunted from breastplate to visor,
Visitors were none the wiser.

Then, one day, the suit went walking,
Past some tourists who were talking.
How they stared with big, round eyes.
Some let out astonished cries!

"This way! Run!" The tour guide said,
And everybody soon had fled.
The empty suit marched down the hall,
And shut the door on one and all!

At night it used its ghostly powers,
To howl from the castle towers.
CLANK, CLANK, CLANK, it stomped around,
And made a spooky creaking sound.

Soon the news spread far and wide
And queues of tourists formed outside.
A great big crowd had come to see,
The clanking ghost that wandered free.

The empty suit was most perplexed
(And not to say a little vexed.)
He'd meant to scare them all away —
And so he left that very day!

Little Ghost Lost

"Come along, Percy," said Mummy. "It's time we took you out on your first proper spooking expedition. And what better night for spooking than Halloween!" "But what do we actually *do* when we go out spooking?" asked Percy.

"Just follow us and copy what we do and you'll soon find out," said Daddy. "But you must remember to stick close, and don't wander off on your own."

With that, Mr and Mrs Ghost and their young son Percy set off on their first night of spooking together. They floated up through the chimney of their home in the Haunted House, and curled out of the top like whisps of smoke. They hovered over the rooftop, then slunk off into the deep, dark night to see what fun they could have.

At the edge of some woods they came to a little cottage, with a fire glowing brightly inside. An old man was heading down the garden path towards the woodpile.

"Follow me," said Daddy. "This will be fun!"

The family of ghosts hid and watched as the old man piled some logs high in his arms. Then with a terrible wail Mr and Mrs Ghost rose up

from behind the woodpile and the old man leapt in the air in fright, sending the wood flying. He ran back to his cottage hollering and screaming, and the ghosts collapsed in giggles.

"That was brilliant!" said Percy.

Next they came to a house with a pumpkin lantern in the window.

"Looks like these folk are entering into the *spirit* of the evening," laughed Mrs Ghost. Peering in through a steamy window, they saw a woman busy baking pumpkin pie. Mr Ghost tapped on the window, and the woman turned to see three ghostly faces pressed against the glass. She threw her arms up and screamed, knocking over a large bag of flour as she did so. The flour puffed up in a big cloud, smothering the poor woman from head to toe.

"She looks pretty ghostly herself, now!" laughed Percy.

All through the evening the family of ghosts scoured the neighbourhood, looking for chances to play their ghostly pranks, jumping out and spooking folk, and squealing with delight as they sent them on their way, screaming. Percy had a great time, and grew braver and bolder at each opportunity, copying his parents' ghastly expressions and gruesome groans.

"I'm a natural at this," thought Percy, smugly. "I bet I could spook someone all on my own!"

Just then he spotted two little children walking ahead of him down a dark street. Percy could not resist the chance to try out his spooking skills on his own, so as soon as his mummy and daddy turned their backs, the naughty little ghost hurried off down the street after the two children. Creeping up behind them, he set his face in its most fearsome expression, got ready to give his most spooky wail, then tapped them on their shoulders. But as the little children spun around Percy froze in horror — instead of the two sweet-faced children he had expected to see, he came eye to eye with two hideously gruesome monsters!

Percy screeched at the top of his voice and fled into the night. He didn't even hear the screams behind him, or see the monsters run home at top speed, where they tore off their Halloween masks and panted out their story to their mother. Poor Percy had never heard of trick-or-treating!

Percy fled down the streets turning this way and that, calling for his mother and father. Where had he left them? He had never been out on his own before, and now all the streets looked the same. Suddenly he felt afraid of the dark. Sinister shadows lurched at him, trees clutched at him with spiky fingers and strange furry monsters hissed at him and swiped him with sharp claws. Poor Percy hurried on through the night — but tonight was the night when witches, wizards, monsters

and ghouls were abroad, and at every turn fresh horrors awaited him. Finally he sank exhausted into a doorway.

"I want my mummy!" he wailed, and began to cry. Before very long he had cried himself to sleep. Hours later he woke with a start. Something was poking and prodding him with a sharp stick.

"What have we here then?" said a mean little voice.

"Looks like a wee ghostie — we can have some fun with him. Let's pinch him!" said another nasty voice. The voices belonged to two goblins — mean, dirty, smelly little goblins, with sharp noses, pointed ears and bony fingers.

"BOO!" said Percy, pulling his most gruesome face. "Leave me alone!"

But the goblins just collapsed in a fit of giggles — it takes a lot to frighten goblins.

"Is that the best you can do?" they taunted and started to poke and pinch poor Percy again. He howled and wailed and pulled all manner of fearsome faces, trying to scare the goblins away, but it just made them laugh all the more and pinch him even harder.

"You can't scare us!" they teased. "Nothing scares us!"

"Oh no?" said a deep voice behind them "How about this!"

The little goblins turned to see two enormous, terrifying ghosts hovering over them ready to pounce. "Help!" they cried as they ran into the night!

"Mummy! Daddy!" cried Percy in delight. "You found me!"

Soon the ghost family were safely back in the Haunted House, and Mrs Ghost was tucking Percy into bed.

"I'm never going to make a good spook!" said Percy miserably.

"Yes you will," soothed Mummy. "After all, you certainly managed to scare us! We were very worried about you. Next time remember to stick close!"

"I promise," said Percy, and in no time at all he was sound asleep, dreaming of ways to spook goblins.

Lonely Hearts

Fun-loving troll, dirty and smelly,
With damp slimy skin and big hairy belly,
Nice muddy fingers and grubby wet toes,
Hot, steamy breath and rings through each nose.

With stains on his shirt and holes in his socks,
Teeth that need cleaning and knots in his locks,
Tears in his trousers and scuffs on his shoe,
He's waiting to meet someone lovely like you.

He likes dirty ditches and hiding in holes,
Is certain to win when he fights other trolls.
Is very attentive, will woo you with roses,
After he's used them to pick both his noses.

He lives on his own, in a dark stinking pit,
Oozing with slime and covered in spit.
Now feeling lonely, he hopes there's a chance
He can meet someone similar for fun and romance!

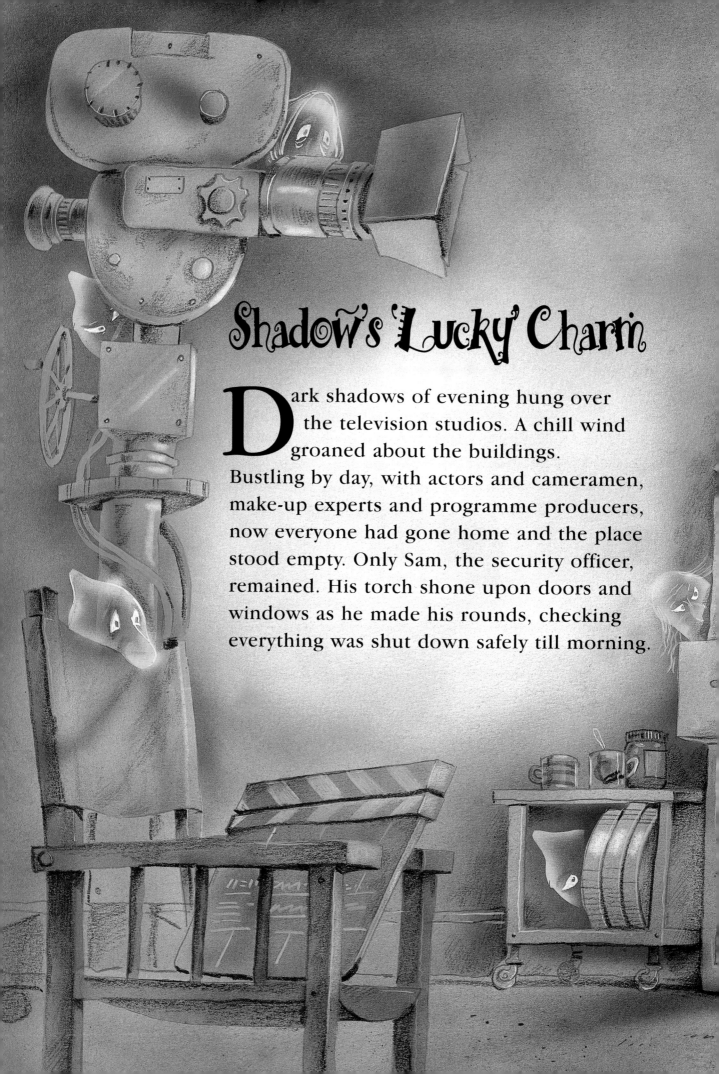

Shadow's 'Lucky' Charm

Dark shadows of evening hung over the television studios. A chill wind groaned about the buildings. Bustling by day, with actors and cameramen, make-up experts and programme producers, now everyone had gone home and the place stood empty. Only Sam, the security officer, remained. His torch shone upon doors and windows as he made his rounds, checking everything was shut down safely till morning.

But as he stepped into Studio One, Sam shivered. Why was it always so cold in there after dark? Sam didn't wait to find out. He felt he was being watched. Shapeless shadows seemed to hover just beyond his torch beam.

Sam was right. He *was* being watched. No sooner had he closed the door and gone on his way, than all manner of phantom forms popped out from behind the studio props...

"Lights, cameras, action!" called Click, a ghostly producer.

Spotlights lit up, cameras focused and the creepiest cast you could ever imagine began to play their parts in another nightly episode of the award-winning spooky soap opera, *Haunted House*, magically transmitted and followed feverishly by ghosts everywhere.

"I can't go on pretending to be a frightening phantom," hissed Grey Ghost, looking into Camera Two. "I just haven't the *spirit* for it!"

"Well, don't tell anybody!" smiled Shadow, delivering her lines in the lead role. "It'll be our secret. Besides..."

Suddenly, she froze. There was a hushed silence as the others looked around in confusion and waited for her to go on. Surely a professional like her hadn't forgotten her lines? After what seemed like a lifetime Shadow continued: "...I've enough ghostly groans, spooky shapes and fearsome faces for the two of us! I'll show you."

Star of the series, Shadow carried on acting as if nothing had happened. Her grimaces were so ghastly, the rest of the cast would have been scared to death, if they were alive!

Meanwhile, in every haunted home across the country, a ghostly audience tuned in to the supernatural series. While humans slept, countless television screens came to life. But only spectres could see the phantom pictures.

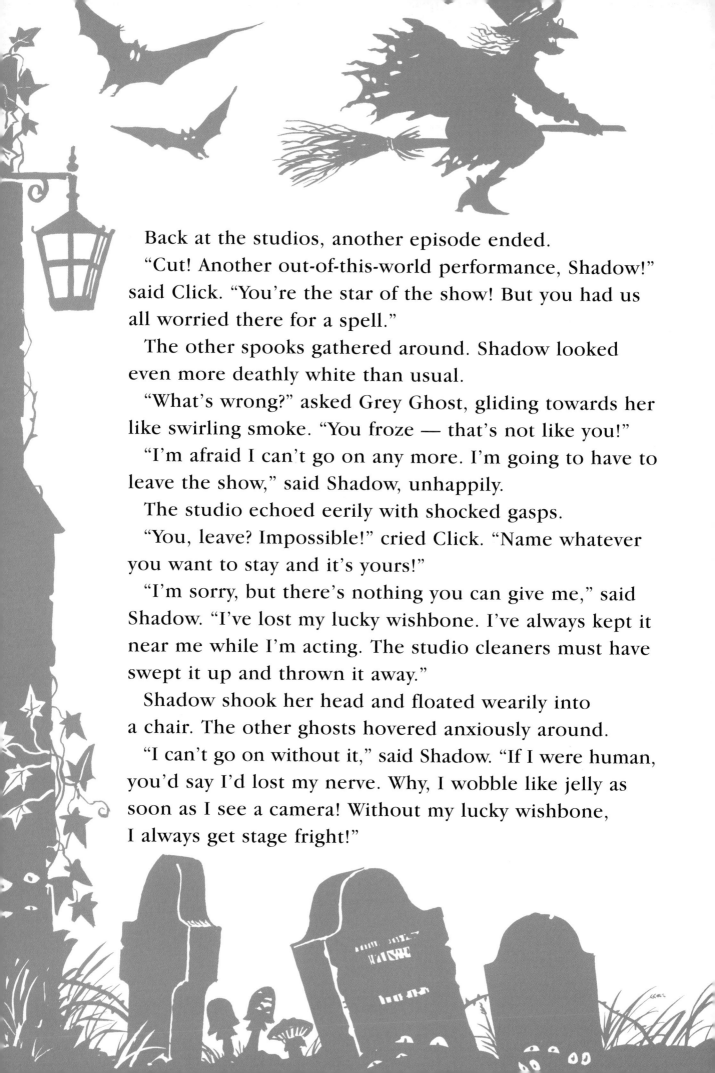

Back at the studios, another episode ended.

"Cut! Another out-of-this-world performance, Shadow!" said Click. "You're the star of the show! But you had us all worried there for a spell."

The other spooks gathered around. Shadow looked even more deathly white than usual.

"What's wrong?" asked Grey Ghost, gliding towards her like swirling smoke. "You froze — that's not like you!"

"I'm afraid I can't go on any more. I'm going to have to leave the show," said Shadow, unhappily.

The studio echoed eerily with shocked gasps.

"You, leave? Impossible!" cried Click. "Name whatever you want to stay and it's yours!"

"I'm sorry, but there's nothing you can give me," said Shadow. "I've lost my lucky wishbone. I've always kept it near me while I'm acting. The studio cleaners must have swept it up and thrown it away."

Shadow shook her head and floated wearily into a chair. The other ghosts hovered anxiously around.

"I can't go on without it," said Shadow. "If I were human, you'd say I'd lost my nerve. Why, I wobble like jelly as soon as I see a camera! Without my lucky wishbone, I always get stage fright!"

Click gently touched Shadow's frosty cheek with a crooked, bony finger.

"You've been working too hard," he smiled. "What you need is a party to cheer you up!"

So the next night as soon as the cameras stopped rolling they threw a huge party for Shadow. The creepy cast did all they could to make her feel better. Two ghosts slipped into a pantomime horse from the costume department and galloped through the air. Then a spectral blob called Slimy slithered about, changing shape. He dripped down the walls and spread like shiny, green goo across the floor. Knuckles, a skeleton, pretended to step on him and slip over.

The ghosts wailed with laughter, all except
Shadow. She kept glancing at the cameras
and worrying about her lost lucky charm.

Next moment, something small stepped
right through the wall near the studio door.
It was the sweetest black cat Shadow had
ever seen. As it trotted towards her, tail
held high, Shadow could see right through
its little body. She was enchanted, and
reached out her hand to stroke it.

"Who are you?" asked Shadow.

"I'm Lucky," purred the cat. "I move as
silently as a shadow."

"Shadow is *my* name!" laughed Shadow.

"Mind if I look round? I've always wanted
to be in a TV show," mewed Lucky.

"I want to be *out* of one," replied Shadow, sadly explaining.

The phantom feline looked thoughtful.

"I've just had a purrrfect idea," said Lucky, and whispered something in Shadow's ear.

When Shadow heard, she let out a spine-chilling shriek of joy. The other ghosts spun round to stare. Even Sam in his office at the far end of the studio buildings sat up with a start from his catnap. He shook his head, yawned and was only too happy to believe he had been dreaming.

"Shadow, are you all right?" asked Grey Ghost, looking worried. .

"I am now," smiled Shadow. "Thanks to my *charming* new friend here, Lucky!"

"Lights, cameras, action!" called Click when filming began again the next night on *Haunted House*.

This time, joining the high-spirited cast of regular spectres, there was an extra ghost. Lucky was delighted to have been given a glide-on part. Shadow was even happier about it. Her faultless performance proved it. After all, Shadow had a new lucky charm. And as for any stage fright, there simply wasn't a *ghost* of a chance it would return now!

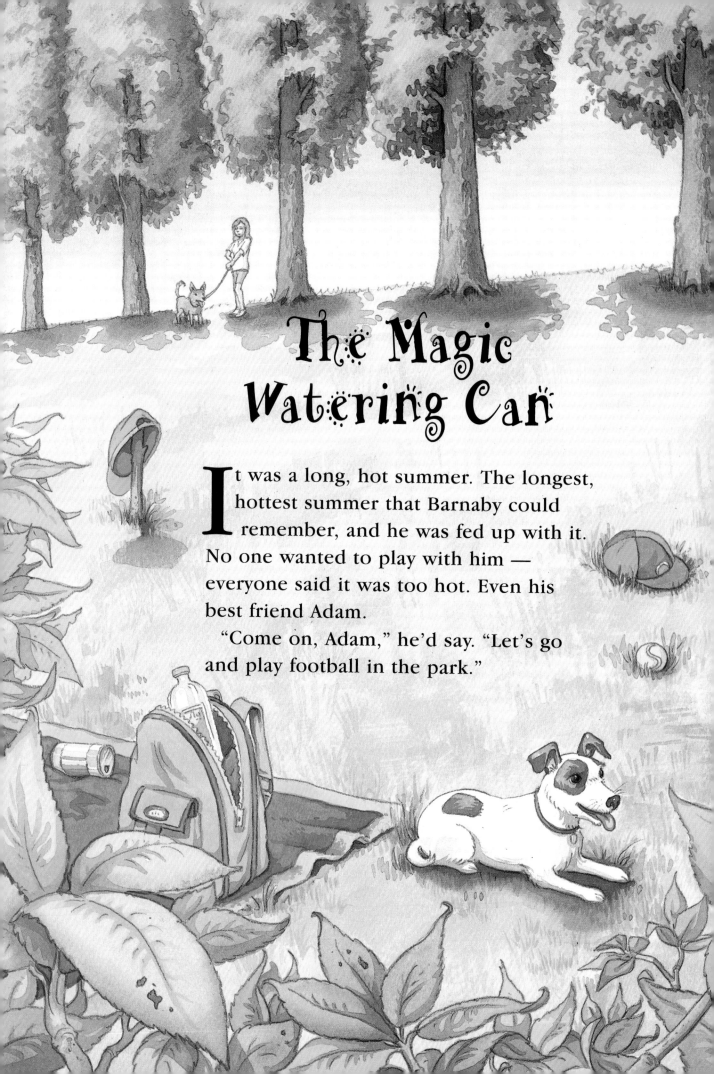

The Magic Watering Can

It was a long, hot summer. The longest, hottest summer that Barnaby could remember, and he was fed up with it. No one wanted to play with him — everyone said it was too hot. Even his best friend Adam.

"Come on, Adam," he'd say. "Let's go and play football in the park."

"It's too hot," Adam would answer. "Let's go swimming." And so they went swimming. But they had been swimming every day for a month and Barnaby was fed up with it.

Then one day his mother told him to get himself ready. They were going to visit Granny. "Yipee!" yelled Barnaby, and rushed to his room to pack. Granny lived in the countryside in a little thatched cottage, surrounded by a beautiful garden full of flowers, and Barnaby loved going to visit her. He would play in the garden for hours, climbing trees, making dens in the bushes, hiding in the long grass, and catching fish in the little stream that ran at the end of the garden. At last he would have something to do!

But when they got to Granny's, what a dismal sight awaited them. The garden was dried up and dusty and bare! The grass was short and brown and scrubby, the bushes were limp and

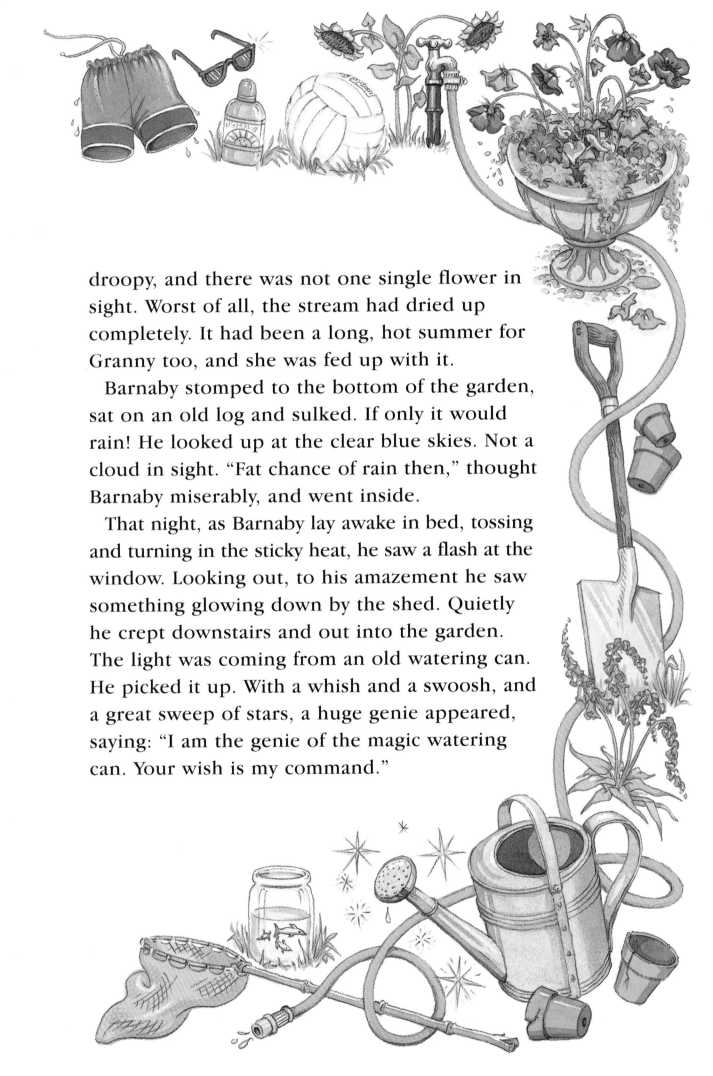

droopy, and there was not one single flower in sight. Worst of all, the stream had dried up completely. It had been a long, hot summer for Granny too, and she was fed up with it.

Barnaby stomped to the bottom of the garden, sat on an old log and sulked. If only it would rain! He looked up at the clear blue skies. Not a cloud in sight. "Fat chance of rain then," thought Barnaby miserably, and went inside.

That night, as Barnaby lay awake in bed, tossing and turning in the sticky heat, he saw a flash at the window. Looking out, to his amazement he saw something glowing down by the shed. Quietly he crept downstairs and out into the garden. The light was coming from an old watering can. He picked it up. With a whish and a swoosh, and a great sweep of stars, a huge genie appeared, saying: "I am the genie of the magic watering can. Your wish is my command."

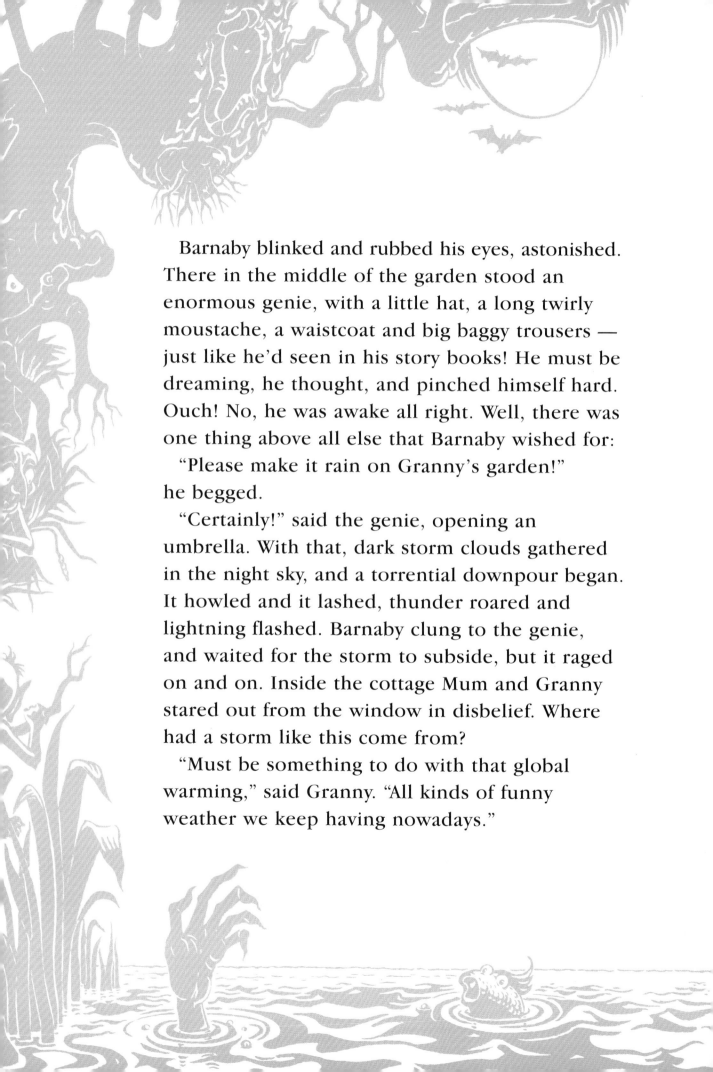

Barnaby blinked and rubbed his eyes, astonished. There in the middle of the garden stood an enormous genie, with a little hat, a long twirly moustache, a waistcoat and big baggy trousers — just like he'd seen in his story books! He must be dreaming, he thought, and pinched himself hard. Ouch! No, he was awake all right. Well, there was one thing above all else that Barnaby wished for:

"Please make it rain on Granny's garden!" he begged.

"Certainly!" said the genie, opening an umbrella. With that, dark storm clouds gathered in the night sky, and a torrential downpour began. It howled and it lashed, thunder roared and lightning flashed. Barnaby clung to the genie, and waited for the storm to subside, but it raged on and on. Inside the cottage Mum and Granny stared out from the window in disbelief. Where had a storm like this come from?

"Must be something to do with that global warming," said Granny. "All kinds of funny weather we keep having nowadays."

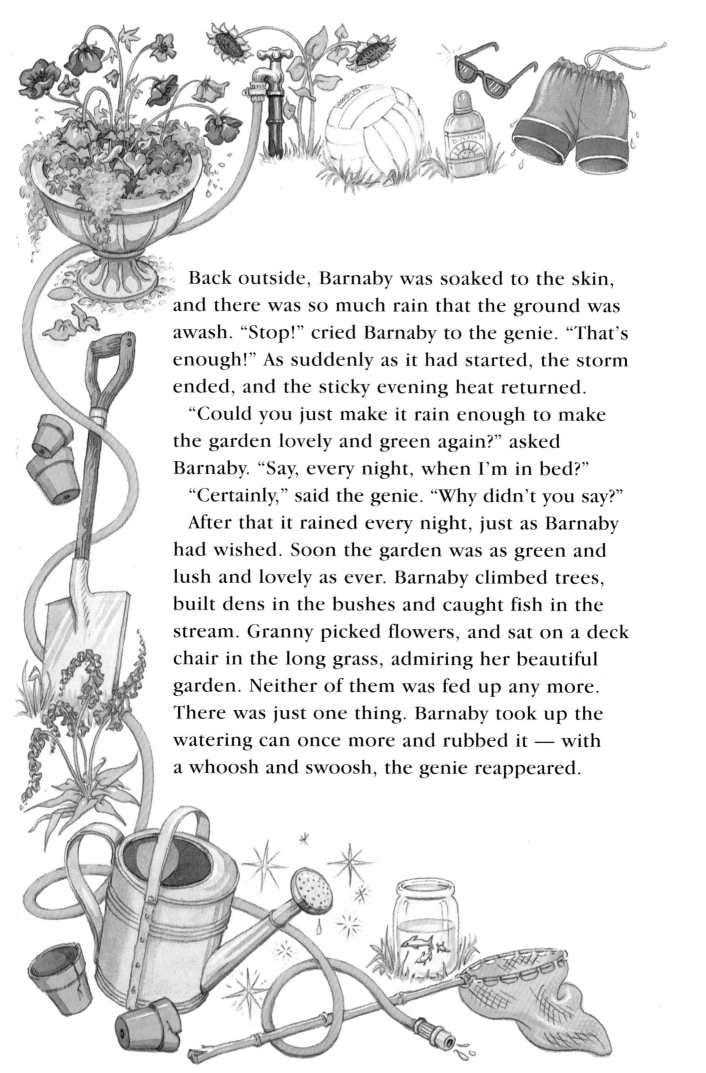

Back outside, Barnaby was soaked to the skin, and there was so much rain that the ground was awash. "Stop!" cried Barnaby to the genie. "That's enough!" As suddenly as it had started, the storm ended, and the sticky evening heat returned.

"Could you just make it rain enough to make the garden lovely and green again?" asked Barnaby. "Say, every night, when I'm in bed?"

"Certainly," said the genie. "Why didn't you say?"

After that it rained every night, just as Barnaby had wished. Soon the garden was as green and lush and lovely as ever. Barnaby climbed trees, built dens in the bushes and caught fish in the stream. Granny picked flowers, and sat on a deck chair in the long grass, admiring her beautiful garden. Neither of them was fed up any more. There was just one thing. Barnaby took up the watering can once more and rubbed it — with a whoosh and swoosh, the genie reappeared.

"I wish my friend Adam was here," said Barnaby. There was a flash and a bang, as Adam appeared, and the genie vanished. Adam blinked and looked around him in amazement. Just then, Mum and Granny came into the garden. They looked at Adam in surprise.

"Hello, Adam!" said Mum. "How did you get here?"

"I have no idea," said Adam, looking around him at the beautiful garden. "But I'm ever so glad I did!"

Time for a Re-vamp!

I'm a vampire in need of a re-vamp,
Just look at the state of my hair!
I've been searching my wardrobe all morning,
But I can't find a thing I can wear!

I'm a vampire in need of a re-vamp,
With too healthy a glow to my skin,
I've been eating so much I've grown podgy,
When we all know vampires should be thin.

I'm a vampire in need of a re-vamp,
The wrinkles are starting to show,

I know I can't help getting older,
But I really have let myself go!

I'm a vampire in need of a re-vamp,
I've been far too busy of late,
There's been so much to sink my teeth into,
I've let myself slip to this state.

I'm a vampire in need of a re-vamp,
So there's only one thing I can do,
Go on telly and have a makeover,
And soon I'll be back good as new!

Spooky Spells

"It's almost Halloween again," said Snitchy Witch to her black cat Treacle. "How the time has flown! And I still haven't quite finished making the food for the Witches Convention. I must do it today."

So she sat down at the table and started to write her shopping list which went something like this: *2 newts; 3 frogs; bag of snails; tin of slug juice; 1 rat's tail; packet of mixed spiders...* She was so busy writing that she didn't notice the little ghost watching her carefully from behind the cauldron...

Now, Halloween, as you all know, is a very special time for witches, and this witch was no exception. In fact, this Halloween was *extra* special for Snitchy Witch as she was hosting the Western Witches Annual Halloween Convention. She was holding it in the ballroom of the Haunted House, hired specially for the occasion. Witches were coming from far and wide to attend lectures on important topics, such as *Magic Brooms and How to Handle Them*; *Growing Warts in a Week* and *If you Want to Get Ahead, Get a Cat!*

The highlight of the event would be a *Spelling Contest*, where the witches would compete for the coveted title of Witch of the Year.

"Just wait until it's my turn," said Snitchy Witch as she finished her list. "I'll show 'em a thing or two!" and she hurried off on her broomstick to the shops.

As soon as he was sure she had gone, Spooky, the little ghost, came out from behind the cauldron. He didn't like stinky witches. Having just one in the Haunted House was bad enough — but a whole convention! It was no use trying to frighten them away — witches weren't afraid of a little ghost like him. But perhaps there was a way to make them scare themselves... Spooky smiled. He would certainly have some fun with those silly old witches...

Snitchy Witch returned from her shopping expedition and spent the rest of the day carefully cooking up the most disgusting food she could think of. Then she dusted off her spellbook and polished up her favourite magic wand. She could hardly wait to demonstrate her spectacular 'garden slug into gigantic gooey chocolate cake' spell! And all the time she was busy preparing, Spooky was busy watching her...

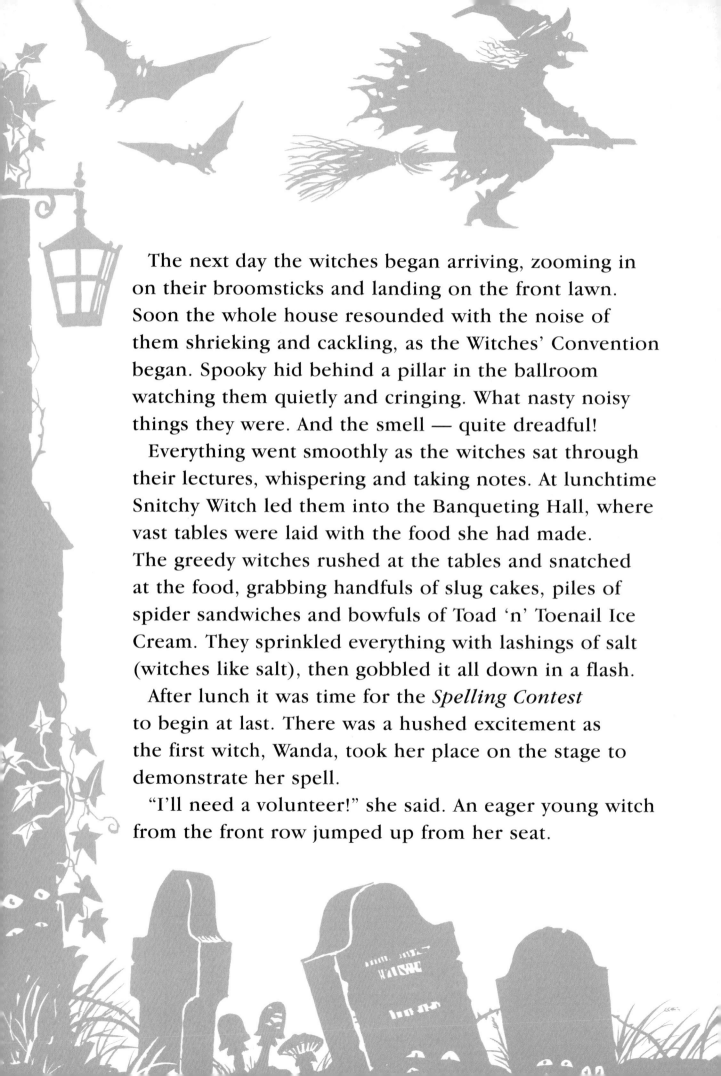

The next day the witches began arriving, zooming in on their broomsticks and landing on the front lawn. Soon the whole house resounded with the noise of them shrieking and cackling, as the Witches' Convention began. Spooky hid behind a pillar in the ballroom watching them quietly and cringing. What nasty noisy things they were. And the smell — quite dreadful!

Everything went smoothly as the witches sat through their lectures, whispering and taking notes. At lunchtime Snitchy Witch led them into the Banqueting Hall, where vast tables were laid with the food she had made. The greedy witches rushed at the tables and snatched at the food, grabbing handfuls of slug cakes, piles of spider sandwiches and bowfuls of Toad 'n' Toenail Ice Cream. They sprinkled everything with lashings of salt (witches like salt), then gobbled it all down in a flash.

After lunch it was time for the *Spelling Contest* to begin at last. There was a hushed excitement as the first witch, Wanda, took her place on the stage to demonstrate her spell.

"I'll need a volunteer!" she said. An eager young witch from the front row jumped up from her seat.

"You're in for a treat!" said Wanda. "I'm going to turn you into a stinking sewer rat! Just temporarily, of course."

"Ooh, lovely," said the young volunteer. "What fun."

Wanda raised her arms, waved her magic wand, and muttered the magic spell:

"She's not the last, she'll be the first, come mystic magic, do your worst!"

The witches watched in eager anticipation, as with a loud bang, a great flash, and a crackle of sparks the volunteer witch transformed before their eyes. But what was this? Instead of becoming a stinking rat, she had changed into a beautiful princess! Wanda looked at her in horror. There's absolutely

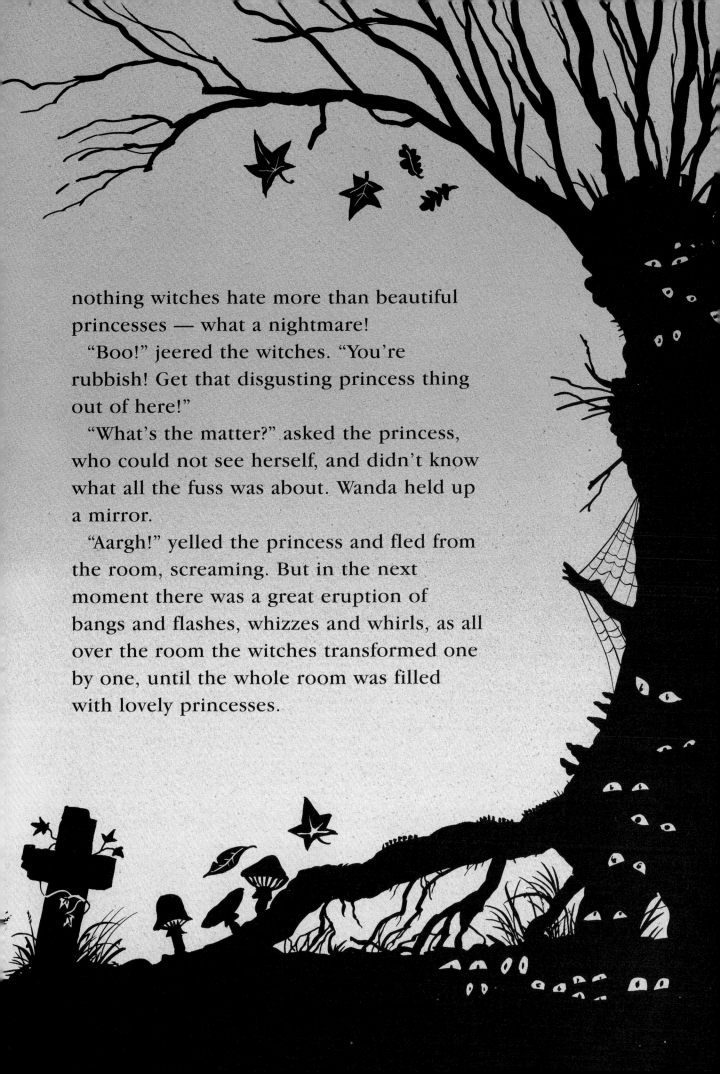

nothing witches hate more than beautiful princesses — what a nightmare!

"Boo!" jeered the witches. "You're rubbish! Get that disgusting princess thing out of here!"

"What's the matter?" asked the princess, who could not see herself, and didn't know what all the fuss was about. Wanda held up a mirror.

"Aargh!" yelled the princess and fled from the room, screaming. But in the next moment there was a great eruption of bangs and flashes, whizzes and whirls, as all over the room the witches transformed one by one, until the whole room was filled with lovely princesses.

Then, what a fuss and commotion! They hollered and screamed and jumped up and down, clutching at their shiny hair and beautiful gowns. Spooky laughed and laughed until he cried, for of course the commotion was all his fault. He had made a spell for beautiful princesses which he had found at the back of Snitchy Witch's spell book while she was out shopping. "Only to be used on your worst enemies, or in emergencies," it had said. Spooky decided this was definitely an emergency, and had added the spell to the salt (which, as you remember, the witches had used plenty of on their lunch!).

Still yelling and screaming (most unladylike!) the princesses leapt on their brooms and fled.

"Come back!" yelled Snitchy Witch (now transformed into a princess herself). "We haven't finished the contest!" But it was no use. The witches, or rather princesses, had gone. Spooky stretched out on an old sofa with a satisfied grin on his face. Peace and quiet once more. Only one stinky witch left in the Haunted House, and even she wasn't too bad now she was a princess!

The Toast Ghost

A hungry ghost wished for some toast,
"I'd eat a loaf!" he'd often boast.
The words he longed someone to utter,
Were "Here's some toast with lots of butter!"

The ghost lived in a ruined house.
He shared it with a little mouse.
It squeaked, "No toast! Don't even look!
There is no cooker, nor a cook!"

The ghost despaired, "What shall I do?"
The mouse replied, "If I were you,
I'd seek a cafe or a restaurant,
Ask them to make the toast you want!"

The ghost soon found the perfect spot.
He dreamed of toast, lovely and hot.
He waited for the cafe to close,
While smells all toasty teased his nose.

He went inside and found the kitchen.
For buttered toast the ghost was itchin'!
Then something white behind the door,
Floated softly to the floor.

The nervous ghost took off in fright –
He found he'd lost his appetite.
"That's really put me off my tea!"
But let me tell, 'tween you and me –
It was the chef's white hat he saw.
That ghost, he don't eat toast no more!

Stand and Deliver

It was a dark and stormy night. Thunder crashed, rain lashed, lightning flashed and, jolting along inside the royal horse and carriage, poor King Penniless felt bruised and bashed!

He had been away on important business, trying unsuccessfully to raise funds to help save his crumbling castle from falling apart. For although he was a king, he was not a wealthy one, having lost all his money in a series of bad investments. He was a kind and gentle king, but he had no head for business. King Penniless leaned back inside his carriage and closed his eyes. What could he do to save himself from ruin?

The royal horse and carriage battled on along the bumpy road that crossed the wild and windy moor. The glass rattled in the carriage windows, and a steady stream of water poured in through a leak in the roof, and dripped onto the king's head.

"What a sorry state to be in," the king thought, miserably. Just then, with a loud whinny, the horses reared up in fright,

and the carriage came crashing to a halt.

"Stand and deliver!" boomed an eerie voice outside. King Penniless nervously lowered the window and peered out into the stormy night, but it was so dark that he couldn't see anything at all. "What's the matter?" the king called to his coachman, trying to sound braver than he felt.

"It.. it's the Gh-ghostly Highwayman!" stuttered his terrified coachman in reply.

"Ghosts, bish-bosh!" called King Penniless, crossly. "It's just the wind. Drive on!"

"I c-can't sir," replied the coachman. "We've lost a wheel."

"Well, hurry up and replace it!" ordered the king. This was all he needed! He was tired and worn out with worry, and he just wanted to get home, put his feet up and have a nice hot cup of cocoa.

The king climbed down out of the carriage to go and see what all the fuss was about for himself. Just then a great flash of lightning lit up the sky, illuminating the moors. And there, right in front of the king, sat the Ghostly Highwayman, perched high upon a pure white horse.

"Stand and deliver — your money or your life!" he cried. His cape swirled around his ashen face, as he pointed an old-fashioned pistol at the king.

Well, the poor king trembled so hard that his teeth started to chatter.

"B..but I d..don't have any money!" he stuttered.

"Nonsense!" cried the Highwayman. "You're the king aren't you?"

"Y-yes — but I'm nearly bankrupt," said the king, and as it seemed there was nothing else for it, he went on to explain his position to his ghostly listener.

By the time the king had finished telling him the story of all his troubles, the Ghostly Highwayman was almost in tears. "How terrible for you," he said. "But there must be some way I can help. Let's think of a plan!"

"Help!" spluttered the king. "Why would you want to help? A moment ago you were threatening to shoot me!"

"I'm sorry. I didn't mean it," said the Ghostly Highwayman. "It's just part of the act. That's what highwaymen are supposed to say. I only stopped your carriage because it's lonely out here, and I wanted someone to talk to."

"Well there are better ways of making friends than waving pistols at people!" said the king, indignantly.

"You're right," said the ghost. "It's just that being a highwayman is all I know, although I was never very good at it — I suppose that's why I got caught. And it was thanks to your great-grandfather that I escaped the gallows, so really I owe you a favour."

He went on to explain how the king's great-grandfather had granted him a royal pardon, after his daughter, the young Princess Angelina,

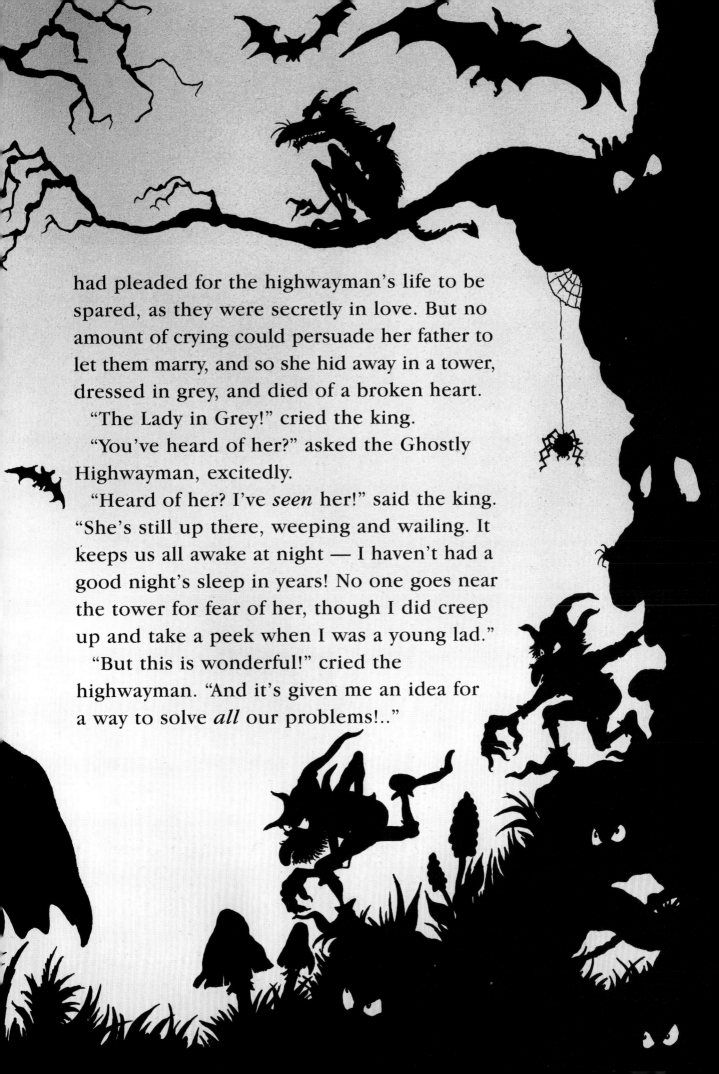

had pleaded for the highwayman's life to be spared, as they were secretly in love. But no amount of crying could persuade her father to let them marry, and so she hid away in a tower, dressed in grey, and died of a broken heart.

"The Lady in Grey!" cried the king.

"You've heard of her?" asked the Ghostly Highwayman, excitedly.

"Heard of her? I've *seen* her!" said the king. "She's still up there, weeping and wailing. It keeps us all awake at night — I haven't had a good night's sleep in years! No one goes near the tower for fear of her, though I did creep up and take a peek when I was a young lad."

"But this is wonderful!" cried the highwayman. "And it's given me an idea for a way to solve *all* our problems!.."

"Stand and deliver! Your money or your life!" boomed the Ghostly Highwayman. The two middle-aged ladies squealed with terror and delight, and quickly handed over their entrance fee for a place on the next tour of the haunted royal castle! The Lady in Grey smiled and winked at the highwayman as she stepped through the wall, let out a ghostly wail, and glided up the staircase. "Follow me!" she called. An eager bunch of tourists clambered up the stairs behind her, watched happily by the king, as he counted the day's takings.

"At this rate, the castle will be restored in no time!" said the king to the Ghostly Highwayman, rubbing his hands together in delight. "How can I ever thank you?"

"Being reunited with the Princess is reward enough," said the Ghostly Highwayman.

"Plus I don't have to live out on that windy moor any longer, holding people up just to have someone to talk to. There's only one thing more I could wish for — Princess Angelina's hand in marriage."

"Brilliant!" said the king. "A ghostly royal wedding. Now that should really bring in the crowds!.."

And as the king settled down to sleep that night, he gave a contented sigh. At last he could sleep in peace!

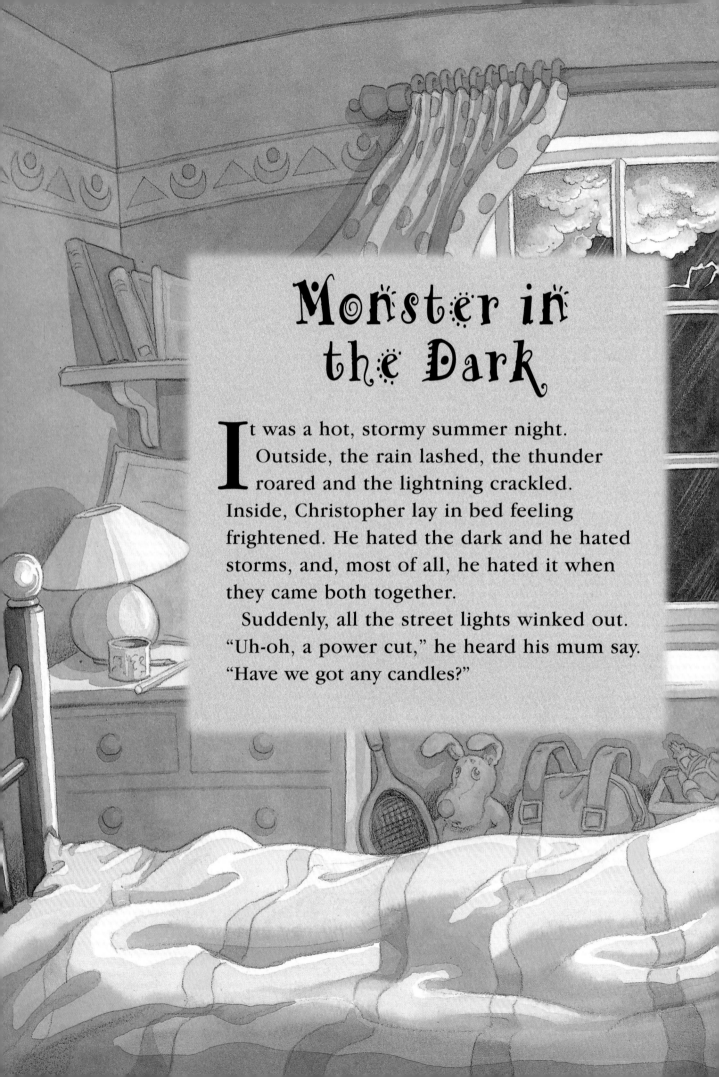

Monster in the Dark

It was a hot, stormy summer night. Outside, the rain lashed, the thunder roared and the lightning crackled. Inside, Christopher lay in bed feeling frightened. He hated the dark and he hated storms, and, most of all, he hated it when they came both together.

Suddenly, all the street lights winked out. "Uh-oh, a power cut," he heard his mum say. "Have we got any candles?"

Christopher cuddled his toy rabbit, pulled the duvet up to his chin and watched the storm flashing outside the window. He blinked. What was that on the windowsill? A dark shape crouched there, lit up by the flashes of lightning. It had gleaming points of light for eyes. Then the dark swallowed it up again. Next time the lightning brightened the sky, the shape was gone.

Christopher's window was open to cool the room, but now he wished it was shut. He was too scared to run over and close it, so he waited, huddled up in his bed, feeling spooked.

There was a thud as one of his books fell off the shelf. Christopher squealed and dived under the duvet.

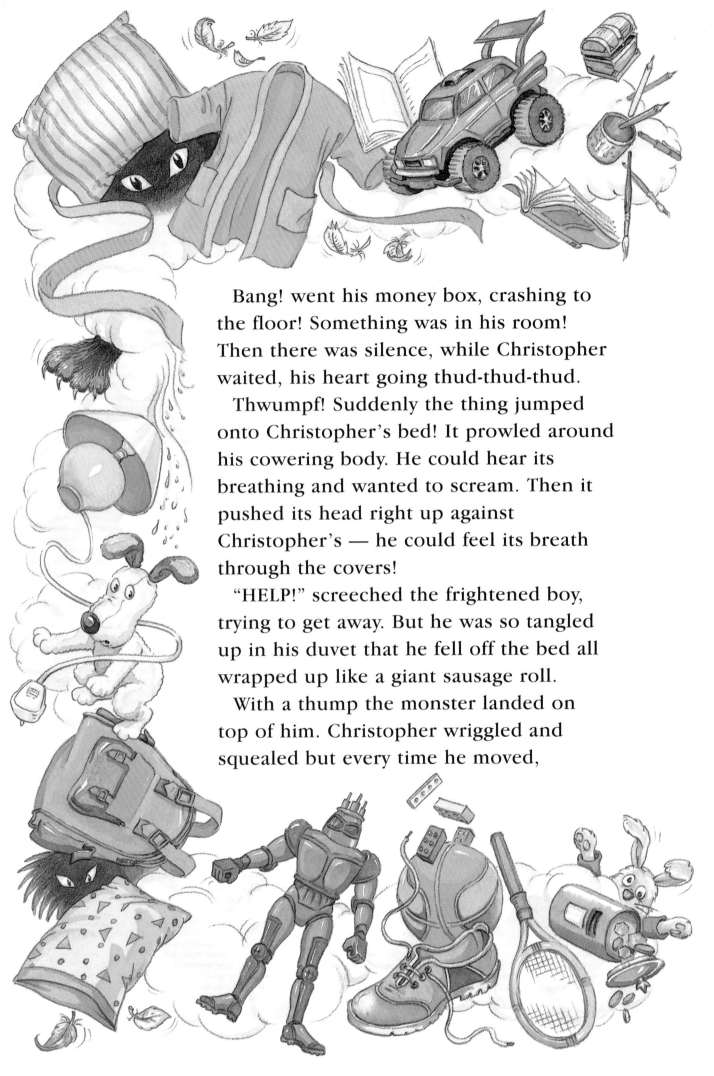

Bang! went his money box, crashing to the floor! Something was in his room! Then there was silence, while Christopher waited, his heart going thud-thud-thud.

Thwumpf! Suddenly the thing jumped onto Christopher's bed! It prowled around his cowering body. He could hear its breathing and wanted to scream. Then it pushed its head right up against Christopher's — he could feel its breath through the covers!

"HELP!" screeched the frightened boy, trying to get away. But he was so tangled up in his duvet that he fell off the bed all wrapped up like a giant sausage roll.

With a thump the monster landed on top of him. Christopher wriggled and squealed but every time he moved,

the creature sank its claws in further.

Poor Christopher was in a frenzy. He had to escape from this terrible beast. Finally he managed to get free of the covers, and went careering round the dark room, crashing into tables and boxes, trying to find the door. Behind him he heard a terrible wailing sound that got louder and louder.

Christopher was actually grateful when a flash of lightning lit up the room, showing him where the door was, and he blundered through it, calling for his parents at the top of his voice.

His mum came running upstairs as fast as she could in the inky blackness, bumping into Christopher where he stood on the dark landing.

"There's a monster in my room," he sobbed. "It was attacking me!"

His mum cuddled him, and while she stood deciding what to do, the lights blinked back on again. Phew! "Oh thank goodness!" cried Christopher.

The noises from his room had stopped. Cautiously, Christopher's mum pushed open his bedroom door.

"Well, what a mess!" she exclaimed. Christopher dare not look. He was hiding behind her in the hallway.

There were feathers floating everywhere, books and toys scattered all over the floor, a broken lamp — and a trail of muddy pawprints right across the carpet.

"What's all this then?" smiled
Christopher's mum, lifting up the duvet.
There, curled up and purring contentedly
was Mac, next door's cat.

"You really *are* a monster," said
Christopher's mum, laughing, and Mac
gave her a big cheesy cat grin to show
that he agreed.

Take the Ghost Train

There's a tumbledown old station,
Where a ghost train waits to go.
All aboard, ghosts, ghouls and goblins,
Watch the engine brightly glow!

In its cab, a phantom fireman,
Helps the engine get up steam.
Chuff-chuff-chuff, it's moving slowly,
Hear its whistle, like a screeeeam!

Ghostly guards are whistling wildly,
Bony fingers wave goodbye,
As along the rails the ghost train glides,
Beneath the moonlit sky.

Witches shriek along the railcars,
While inside the dining car,
Vampires munch and crunch with monsters,
Sipping cocktails at the bar!

On they speed through misty marshes,
What a chilling sight to see.
Ghostly faces at the windows,
Silent wheels turn eerily!

If there were tickets for the ghost train,
Would you dare to take a ride?
Or would you quickly run away,
And find somewhere to hide!

The Little Monster

There was once a boy called Timothy Hogwash. With a name like Timothy he should have been a very nice little boy. But he wasn't. He was horrible. He was lazy and naughty and he never did anything his mum told him. You should have seen his bedroom. His toys were all over the place, and his favourite game was to jump on them and break them. Then he'd howl and say, "I want a new one!"

He left the drawers in his chest of drawers hanging open, with socks and vests poking out. His poor mum kept tidying them, but Timothy just pulled them all out again.

On the floor were bits of old beefburger, sucked-a-little-bit sweets, spilt drinks, half-eaten cheese sandwiches and other yucky, squidgy things. Some of them had gone all green and furry.

His mum said she wasn't going to clean his room any more. She said, "It's your job to tidy your room, Timothy." But he took no notice.

One day Timothy went too far. It all began when his mum said, "If you don't tidy your room, there'll be no tea for you tonight."

Now, it happened to be a Tuesday. And on Tuesdays, Timothy's mum always made egg sandwiches with strawberry trifle, which was Timothy's favourite tea.

So Timothy got cross. He got so cross his face went red and then purple. He got so cross that his hands made little fists and his knees bumped together.

"Shan't!" said Timothy.

And he ran upstairs, and slammed his bedroom door, very, very hard. He pulled all the clothes out of his drawers. Then he jumped up and down on his favourite plastic truck. Then he poured his strawberry milkshake onto the rug by the side of his bed. I told you he was really horrible.

Now, Timothy was so exhausted by all this bad behaviour that he felt rather tired. So he lay down on his bed and in no time at all he was fast asleep.

Much later, Timothy woke up. He felt hungry and thirsty, and decided to go downstairs to get a drink and a biscuit.

So he went to open the door — but it simply wouldn't open.

"Go away." said the door.

Timothy nearly jumped out of his skin.

"I must be dreaming," he said to himself and shook his head. Then he tried to open the door once again.

"If you don't leave me alone," said the door, "I'm going to swing open and give you a good smack."

Timothy's lower lip started to tremble. He didn't like this stupid dream one bit. So he tried to get back into bed. But something was stopping him! Something was holding onto his ankle very tight. By the light of the moon through his window, Timothy saw what it was.

It was a pink, slimy, furry, slobbering, bug-eyed blob on the floor, and it was chattering to itself very fast. It was very smelly, and it shivered and quivered and waved it's strawberry-coloured arms about. It curled itself around Timothy's leg. And it wouldn't let go.

"Don't stand on me you horrid boy!" it chattered. "Or I'll teach you a lesson you won't forget!"

And the pink monster began to pull Timothy's legs from under him...

Timothy was scared. Very, very scared. He tried to grab onto one of the open drawers. And what do you think!? It slammed shut till Timothy's hand was stuck fast.

"Oh no you don't!" said the drawer in a very squeaky voice. "You threw out all those nice woolly socks that kept me warm. Now I'm all cold and lonely. You must stay and keep me company."

Then Timothy heard a vroom, vroom, like an engine. It was very loud.

And getting louder! He turned around and saw his plastic truck.

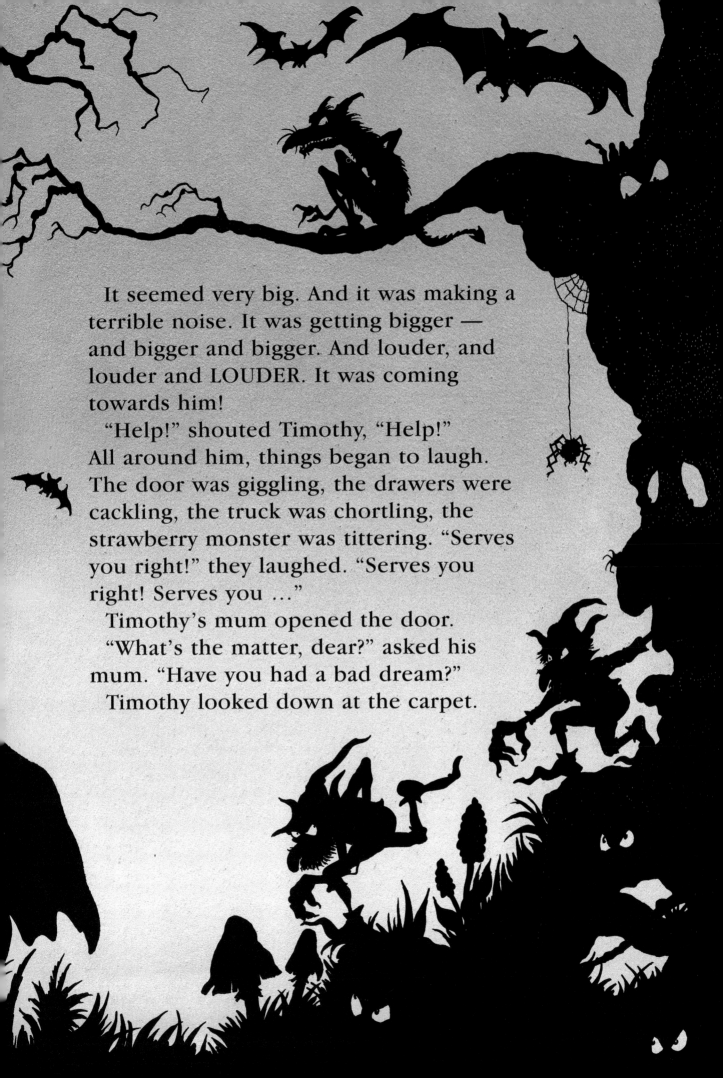

It seemed very big. And it was making a terrible noise. It was getting bigger — and bigger and bigger. And louder, and louder and LOUDER. It was coming towards him!

"Help!" shouted Timothy, "Help!" All around him, things began to laugh. The door was giggling, the drawers were cackling, the truck was chortling, the strawberry monster was tittering. "Serves you right!" they laughed. "Serves you right! Serves you …"

Timothy's mum opened the door.

"What's the matter, dear?" asked his mum. "Have you had a bad dream?"

Timothy looked down at the carpet.

His feet were all wet. He was standing on his socks that were all covered in strawberry milkshake.

Timothy's mum saw his hand in the drawer and smiled.

"What a good boy you are, Timothy!" she beamed. "But there's no need to tidy your drawers now, dear. Leave it until the morning."

Timothy's mouth opened. Then it closed again. He could swear that the plastic truck had moved nearer.

His mum tucked him up in bed. "Leave the door open, Mum!" he said. Then he lay there, wide awake, all night.

Next day he got up early and tidied his room. He put all his toys in the toybox. He put all his clothes neatly back in the drawers. He carefully mended his plastic truck. And he scrubbed his little rug till it was squeaky clean.

"Sorry, door," he said to the door.
"Sorry, drawers," he said to the drawers.
"Sorry, truck," he said to the truck.
"Sorry, Mum," he said to his mum.
And after that Timothy's room was always tidy. And Timothy always did what he was told. (Nearly).

Phantom Footsteps

Phantom footsteps in the hallway,
The heavy door creaks open wide,
A creepy voice speaks out of nowhere:
"Step this way, do come inside."

Candles flicker in the darkness,
A floating lantern leads the way,
Down silent hall and empty passage,
Cold draughts blow and shadows play.

Cobwebs stretch from every corner,
Overhead hang sleeping bats,
Portraits watch as you creep by them,
On the floor run squeaking rats!

The lantern leads into the great hall,
Dimly lit by candlelight,
Empty, but for one large coffin —
What a dreaded, fearful sight!

As you approach the lid creaks open,
A ghostly figure smiles at you,
Holds out a hand, and bids you welcome —
"Have some tea, one lump or two?"

It's good to make friends with your neighbours,
For who knows what could be in store,
So don't refuse an invitation,
If a *vampire* moves next door!

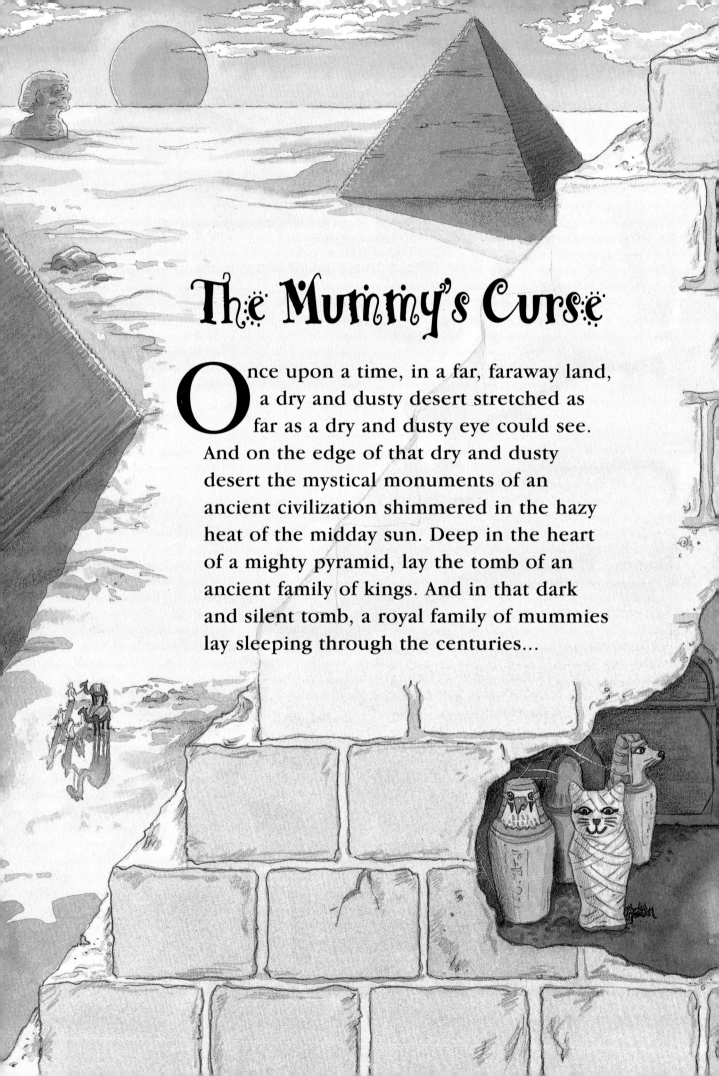

The Mummy's Curse

Once upon a time, in a far, faraway land, a dry and dusty desert stretched as far as a dry and dusty eye could see. And on the edge of that dry and dusty desert the mystical monuments of an ancient civilization shimmered in the hazy heat of the midday sun. Deep in the heart of a mighty pyramid, lay the tomb of an ancient family of kings. And in that dark and silent tomb, a royal family of mummies lay sleeping through the centuries...

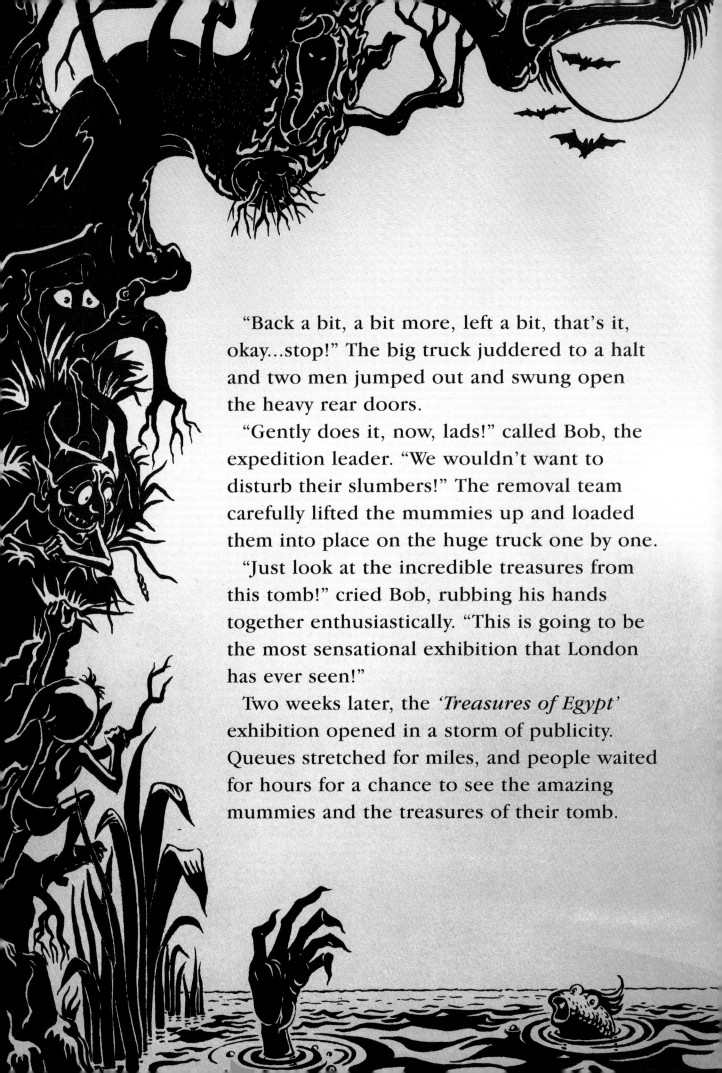

"Back a bit, a bit more, left a bit, that's it, okay...stop!" The big truck juddered to a halt and two men jumped out and swung open the heavy rear doors.

"Gently does it, now, lads!" called Bob, the expedition leader. "We wouldn't want to disturb their slumbers!" The removal team carefully lifted the mummies up and loaded them into place on the huge truck one by one.

"Just look at the incredible treasures from this tomb!" cried Bob, rubbing his hands together enthusiastically. "This is going to be the most sensational exhibition that London has ever seen!"

Two weeks later, the *'Treasures of Egypt'* exhibition opened in a storm of publicity. Queues stretched for miles, and people waited for hours for a chance to see the amazing mummies and the treasures of their tomb.

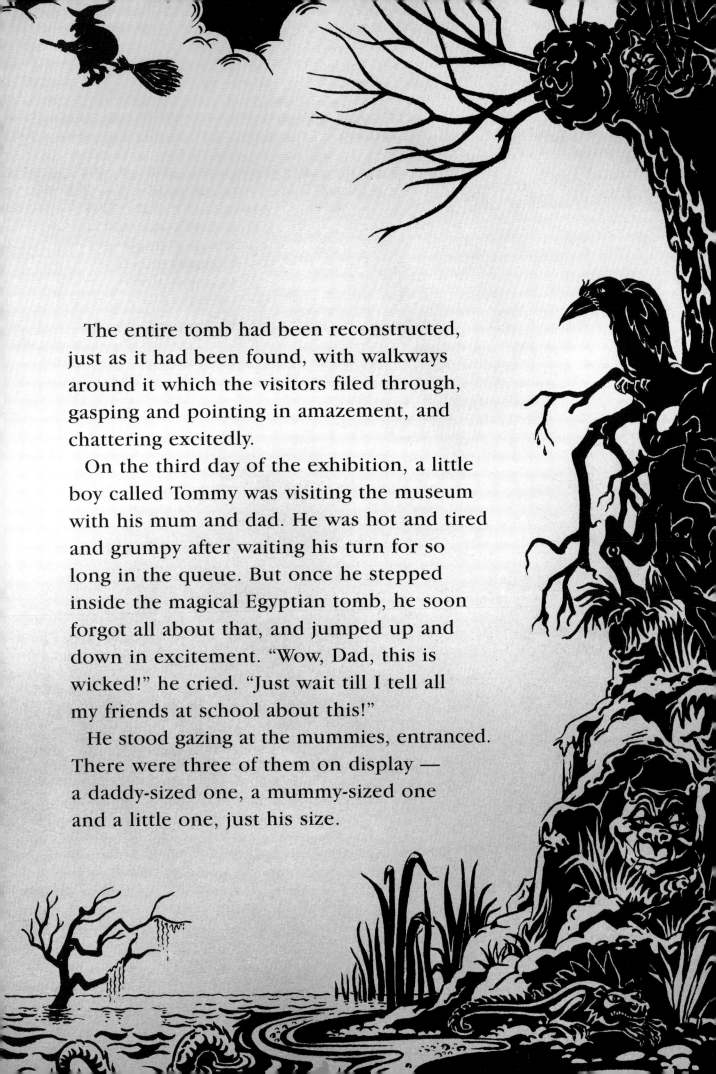

The entire tomb had been reconstructed, just as it had been found, with walkways around it which the visitors filed through, gasping and pointing in amazement, and chattering excitedly.

On the third day of the exhibition, a little boy called Tommy was visiting the museum with his mum and dad. He was hot and tired and grumpy after waiting his turn for so long in the queue. But once he stepped inside the magical Egyptian tomb, he soon forgot all about that, and jumped up and down in excitement. "Wow, Dad, this is wicked!" he cried. "Just wait till I tell all my friends at school about this!"

He stood gazing at the mummies, entranced. There were three of them on display — a daddy-sized one, a mummy-sized one and a little one, just his size.

Then, as Tommy stood there trying to imagine what life must have been like in Ancient Egypt, something very strange happened. The little mummy opened one eye, looked from side to side then shut it again, fast. Tommy blinked, and rubbed his eyes in astonishment.

Tommy thought that he must be seeing things! He looked again, and the little mummy opened its eyes, winked at him, then shut them tight.

"Mum! Dad!" cried Tommy, pulling at their sleeves in excitement. "The little mummy winked at me!"

"Please don't be silly, dear," said Mummy. "Mummies can't wink."

"Your imagination is running away with you, son," laughed Daddy, and he tousled Tommy's hair affectionately. Tommy knew it was no use trying to convince them, as he could hardly believe it himself.

He wanted to stay and see if the little mummy would open his eyes again, but there was a big crowd behind him and he had to move along.

Meanwhile, the little mummy was feeling hot and tired and very confused himself. He had woken up in the night and looked around inside the tomb. It seemed as though he had been asleep forever. He yawned and stretched. He could see his mummy and daddy lying alongside him. Better wait for them to wake up too, so he laid back down and went to sleep.

Next morning the little mummy had been woken by a lot of noise. He opened one eye — who were all these odd-looking people, with strange bright-coloured garments, all staring at him and pointing? He shut his eye again fast. But just to make sure he wasn't seeing things he opened both his eyes again.

A little boy was standing right in front of him, looking at him in amazement. He looked friendly, so the mummy winked at him, then shut his eyes again tight. Perhaps if he stayed very still they would all go away.

But they didn't go away. The noise got louder and louder, and the little mummy got hotter and hotter. He felt stiff and uncomfortable and he was dying to stretch his legs. He took one more peek and decided the strange people looked friendly enough, so he plucked up his courage and with a great creak he climbed out of his case.

Well, there was pandemonium! People screamed and ran, some fainted, others stood frozen to the spot. Someone pulled the fire alarm and guards came running from every corner. The little mummy was terrified — whatever was going on? He ran from the room and out into the museum, his bandages trailing behind him. People screeched and fled, scattering in all directions as he came running towards them.

Sitting in the coffee shop with his mum and dad, Tommy watched as the little mummy ran past heading for the section on Ancient China.

"I told you he winked!" said Tommy to his astonished parents, leaping up from the table. Nearby, the museum guards were all arguing about who should try to catch the little mummy. No one wanted to volunteer.

"I'll go," said Tommy and, before anyone could stop him, he raced off in the direction the little mummy had taken. He had to search through Ancient China, South America, India and Greece before he found him hiding inside a Roman temple.

"Where am I? I want my mummy!" said the mummy, starting to cry.

"Don't worry," said Tommy. "I'll take you to her!" Tommy led the little mummy back, trying to explain where they were. The poor mummy was very confused, as everything looked so odd. Crowds cowered behind statues and pillars as they passed, marvelling at Tommy's bravery.

Before long the little mummy was back in his tomb. "I want to go home!" he said to Tommy.

"Just climb in your case and go back to sleep, and I'm sure you'll soon be there," said Tommy.

And that is just what happened. Scientists came from all over the world, but though they poked and prodded, and did all kinds of tests, nothing would make the little mummy wake up again. The exhibition was closed, and soon the mummies were back in Egypt, restored to their tomb. Tommy became a national hero and had his picture in all the newspapers.

And as for Bob, the expedition leader? "That exhibition certainly was sensational!" he said.

The Wrong Cat

"I need three dead mice for this spell, Grazelgritch. Go and catch them," said Witch Yukspell, shoving her black cat out of the door.

Poor Grazelgritch – it was freezing cold outside and a nasty sleety rain had started. He headed for the woods and sat under a holly bush waiting for a mouse to pass by.

"Hello," said a voice behind him. "Is this a good place to catch mice?" He turned to see another black cat crouching under the holly. Grazelgritch thought she was beautiful.

"Who are you?" he asked. "I've never seen you in the woods before."

"I'm Alice," said the other cat. "I live over the other side of the hill. I thought I'd see a bit more of the neighbourhood, have an adventure. What's your name?"

"Grazelgritch," said the witch's cat. Alice snorted.

"What kind of a name is that?!" she laughed.

"A magic name," said Grazelgritch. "I work for a witch. I'm the seventh kitten of a seventh kitten, born on Halloween night, so I've got magic properties. That's why I'm owned by Yukspell. And I wish I wasn't."

"A witch's cat!" said Alice. "How exciting."

"It's not. It's horrible. Yukspell treats me like dirt, sending me out in all weathers, half-starving me. I have to sleep in the draughtiest room in that rickety old house. And what's more, she smells!"

"You poor thing," said Alice. "I lead a very boring life – sleeping most of the day, eating tinned food, leftovers if I'm lucky. I have to go to the vet sometimes."

"Sounds like heaven," sighed Grazelgritch, nibbling at a flea between his toes.

"Well, why don't we swap for a while?" suggested Alice. "Go on – have a holiday. And I can have my adventure!"

Grazelgritch thought she must be bonkers but he agreed at once, and Alice took the dead mice they caught to the witch's house on the hill.

"About time too!" snapped Yukspell, grabbing the mice and flinging them into the cauldron. "You look fatter. How many mice did you gobble up before you brought these home, you idle, greedy, useless cat?!"

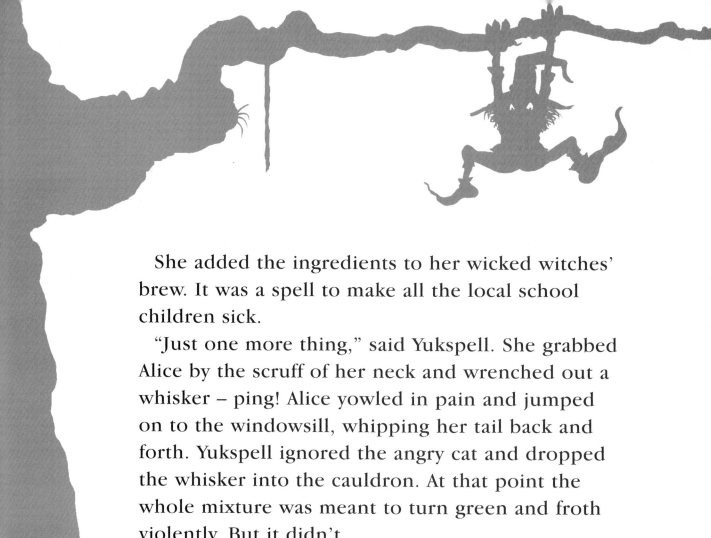

She added the ingredients to her wicked witches' brew. It was a spell to make all the local school children sick.

"Just one more thing," said Yukspell. She grabbed Alice by the scruff of her neck and wrenched out a whisker – ping! Alice yowled in pain and jumped on to the windowsill, whipping her tail back and forth. Yukspell ignored the angry cat and dropped the whisker into the cauldron. At that point the whole mixture was meant to turn green and froth violently. But it didn't.

"Funny," said the witch, checking her spell book. Of course the problem was that Alice was an ordinary cat – the fourth kitten in a litter of six, born at Easter – not a magic cat at all. Yukspell was furious. Four hours work wasted.

"Grazelgritch!" she screeched. "Were those mice or voles?!" She turned and stared at the black cat. Then slowly the truth dawned on Yukspell.

"An imposter!" she screamed. "You're not Grazelgritch!" She grabbed Alice and threw her out of the window.

"You're lucky I didn't put you in the cauldron!" she shouted after the poor cat, as Alice raced away down the hill.

When Alice got home, she found Grazelgritch purring contentedly on her owner's lap.

"Oh no! That was quick!" he said. "Do I have to go back so soon? I haven't had supper yet."

"I don't think I'd make a good adventurer," said Alice. "But it's all right, don't go. My owners said just the other day that they'd like to give a home to another cat to keep me company. Well, I choose you!"

Yukspell was furious that Grazelgritch had deserted her. Without a magic cat none of her spells worked any more, which made life a lot more pleasant for everyone else who lived around her. She had to content herself with scaring people on her broomstick.

Alice's owners were happy to give a home
to her new friend. And wouldn't you know it?
The following autumn, Alice had seven sooty
black kittens. But Grazelgritch chose the new
home for the youngest kitten very carefully –
it went to live with a very nice family in the
town. They never knew that they owned a
magical cat, and that's exactly how
Grazelgritch wanted it.

Ode to Ghosts

A ghost he has a sad old life
   Haunting empty castles.
   On birthdays and at Christmas time
The postman brings no parcels.

He floats around from room to room,
He howls and clanks his chains.
But everyone ignores the noise,
And blames it on the drains.

And if by chance he should appear
Most people scream with fright.
He just can't understand it —
Is he *such* a dreadful sight?

He has no friends to play with
It really is a shame.
He'd like to come around for tea,
Or join you in a game.

But people think that ghosts are bad
And so they stay away.
There's no-one he can natter to,
Or pass the time of day.

So if you ever meet a ghost
Don't run away in fright.
Stay awhile and have a chat,
You'll find they're most polite.

All Done and Dusted

Duster was a witch's cat. He came from a long line of witches' cats, a fact of which he was very proud, for he and his ancestors were known far and wide to be very fine witches' cats indeed. He lived in a little cottage with a kind witch called Mavis, of whom he was very fond. Mavis thanked her lucky stars for Duster, and told him often that he was the best cat a witch could wish for. So you would think that Duster would be happy and content, but he wasn't. You see, Duster had a problem – and a rather mucky problem at that.

Now, as you know, cats are clean and tidy creatures. They wash at least ten times a day, and are carefully groomed at all times. They are light on their feet and can tiptoe across crowded surfaces without making a sound or knocking anything over.

But witches are a completely different matter. They only wash twice a year (Christmas and birthdays). They crash about, knocking things over (like pots of sticky green slime), and they never wash anything up after using it. And of all the grimy, slimy, mucky, messy witches, Mavis was the worst. Only that morning Duster had used up another one of his nine lives when he slipped in a pool of snail slime on the floor, tripped over Mavis' broomstick, that as usual had been left lying on the floor, and was catapulted across the room, narrowly missing the bubbling cauldron on the fire. Poor Duster was at the end of his tether.

So it was with a heavy heart that he sat thinking how to celebrate his birthday, which was in a few days time. He wanted to have a few friends over, but the cottage was in such a mess that he felt too embarrassed. But while he was pondering what to do, Mavis suddenly announced that she had to go and visit her sister, Ethel for a few days.

Apparently, Ethel had cast a spell to turn everything she touched into chocolate, but as it was the middle of summer her whole cottage was melting into one big sticky mess.

"It's very kind of you to go and help Ethel tidy up," said Duster.

"Oh, I can't wait," said Mavis, loading her bags onto her broomstick. "Every witch in the forest will be there, it will be a real party."

"I don't understand," said Duster, watching Mavis from the safety of the window sill. "None of you are exactly good at housework."

"Housework!" Mavis spluttered. "Who said anything about *housework*? We're not going to *clean* her house — we're going to *eat* it!" she chuckled, licking her lips and patting her round belly. "We'll make chocolate custard, chocolate mousse, chocolate cake, chocolate chip cookies..." And still muttering about chocolate, she hopped on her broomstick and flew away.

Duster tutted in disapproval. The only time witches cleared anything up was when there was food involved, which is why all witches have very clean fridges.

As Duster tucked himself into bed that night an idea came to him. While Mavis was at her sister's, he could clean up the cottage and invite his friends over for a birthday tea. After all, many springs had come and gone without a clean — it was high time he took action!

The next morning, Duster got up bright and early, put on his apron and got straight to work. First of all he cleared everything into the garden so that he could see what he was doing. He swept the floor and polished it till it shone. Then he scrubbed the table and covered it with a nice clean tablecloth. Next, he dusted the bookshelves, being careful not to open the spellbooks in case any magic fell out.

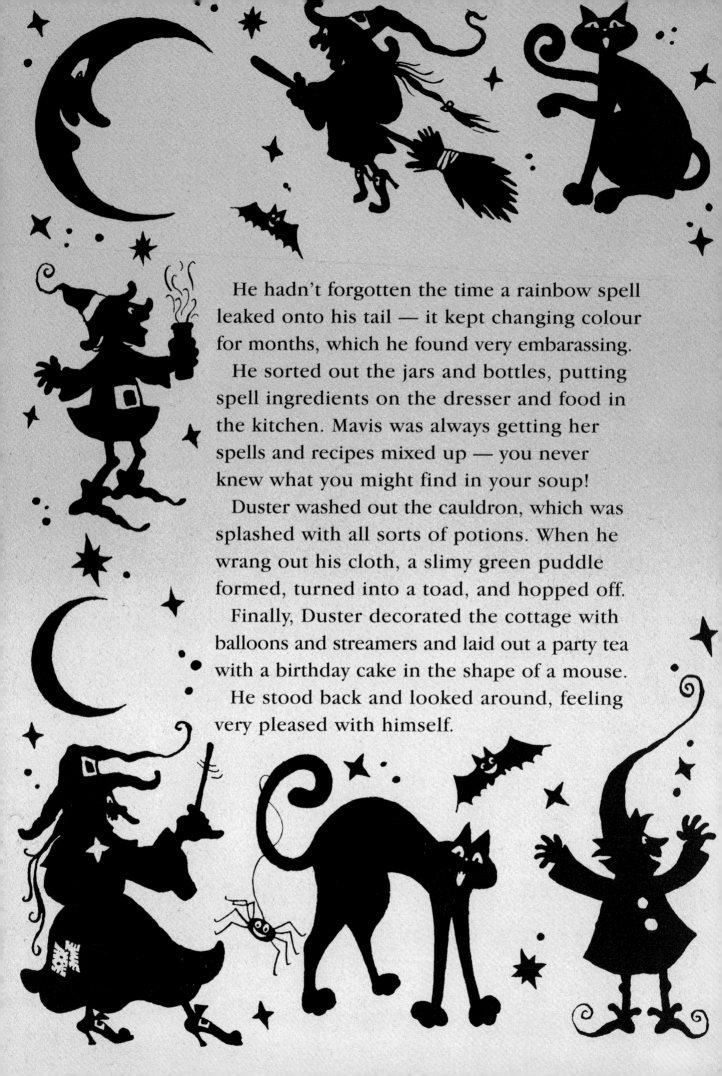

He hadn't forgotten the time a rainbow spell leaked onto his tail — it kept changing colour for months, which he found very embarassing.

He sorted out the jars and bottles, putting spell ingredients on the dresser and food in the kitchen. Mavis was always getting her spells and recipes mixed up — you never knew what you might find in your soup!

Duster washed out the cauldron, which was splashed with all sorts of potions. When he wrang out his cloth, a slimy green puddle formed, turned into a toad, and hopped off.

Finally, Duster decorated the cottage with balloons and streamers and laid out a party tea with a birthday cake in the shape of a mouse.

He stood back and looked around, feeling very pleased with himself.

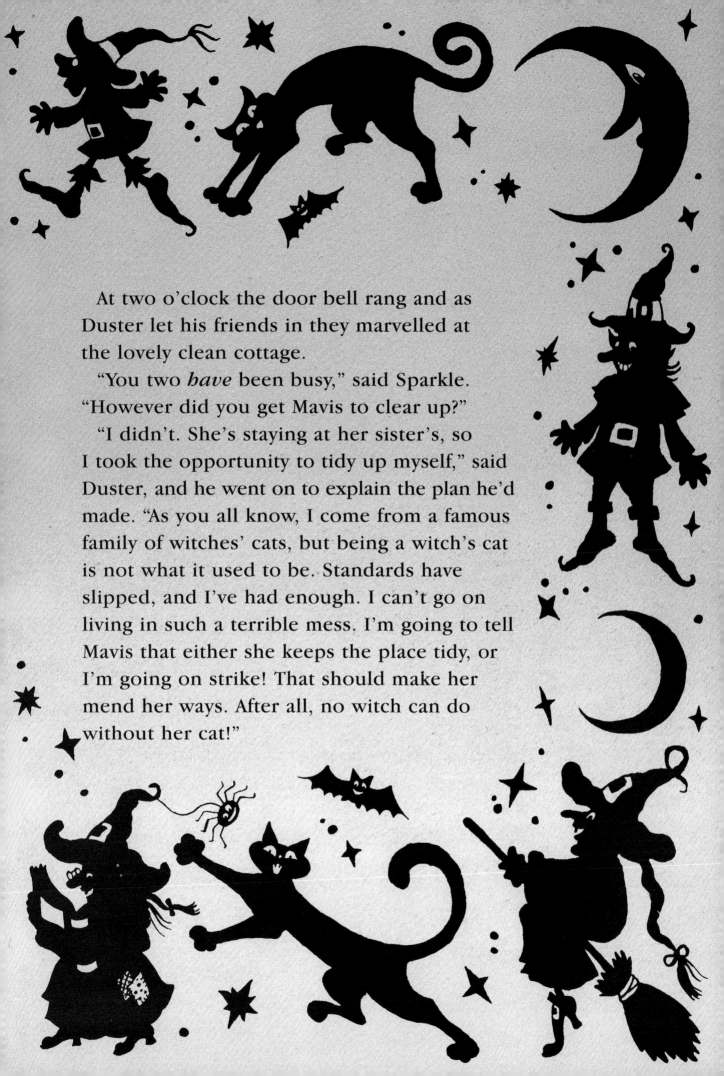

At two o'clock the door bell rang and as Duster let his friends in they marvelled at the lovely clean cottage.

"You two *have* been busy," said Sparkle. "However did you get Mavis to clear up?"

"I didn't. She's staying at her sister's, so I took the opportunity to tidy up myself," said Duster, and he went on to explain the plan he'd made. "As you all know, I come from a famous family of witches' cats, but being a witch's cat is not what it used to be. Standards have slipped, and I've had enough. I can't go on living in such a terrible mess. I'm going to tell Mavis that either she keeps the place tidy, or I'm going on strike! That should make her mend her ways. After all, no witch can do without her cat!"

"Good for you, that's the idea!" cheered the others.

"If only we could all do the same!" said Sweep.

"But we can!" cried Bristle. "All the witches have gone to Ethel's. We can *all* clean our cottages!" The cats all nodded excitedly, and happily discussed their cleaning plans while enjoying the birthday tea.

A few days later, Mavis came hurtling through the door on her broomstick, but she stopped in her tracks when she saw the cottage.

"Oh my, what have you done? Where are all my things? cried Mavis.

"It's all right, they're all here. I've just tidied them up," said Duster, opening cupboards and showing her. "There are going to be a few changes around here from now on," he went on firmly, and explained his ultimatum to Mavis. All over the forest the other cats were doing just the same.

After much grumbling and complaining, Mavis sulkily agreed to keep tidy. "But I still liked it better messy," she muttered.

"Too late!" said Duster. "It's all done and dusted! Now let's have a nice cup of tea." And from then on, Duster was a very happy witch's cat indeed.

The Monster Marching Band

Oompah, oompah goes the trombone,
Held tight in a bony hand.
Boom, boom, boom the bass drum thunders.
Meet the Monster Marching Band!

Through dark streets, past silent houses,
Phantoms march as bold as brass,
Piping pipes and trumping trumpets,
Clashing cymbals as they pass.

Sleepy folk peep out through curtains
Wondering what's disturbed their rest,
But here's the stuff of their worst nightmares —
A sight they never could have guessed!

Ghoulish fingers clutch at drumsticks,
Zombies march past with glazed eyes,
Vampires play on tuneless tubas,
Mummies blow horns to the skies.

A spectral player sounds the bugle,
Ghastly ghosts play clarinets,
On they march past church and graveyard,
Led by phantom majorettes!

So if you ever chance to hear them,
Marching through your town at night,
Just stay put beneath your covers,
Or you'll be in for a fright!

A Brush with Danger

Lydia liked going to her grandparents'. She called them Janny and Grumps and liked staying with them because they had a big garden and a friendly dog called Max.

The morning after she arrived, Janny asked Lydia to take some peelings down to the compost heap.

"Do I have to?" said Lydia because she knew that a monster lived in the compost heap.

"Old Composti won't hurt you," laughed Janny. "Take Max with you if you are worried, but please don't go in the woodshed — it's not a safe place for children."

So Lydia skipped down the path, past the pretty flowerbeds, past the vegetable patch, past the chickens and down, down to the bottom of the garden, where a bendy tree leaned over an old rickety ramshackle shed. Next to it was the compost heap, where Composti Monster lived. He was very useful for Janny, gobbling up all the peelings and dead leaves, grass cuttings and hedge trimmings, turning them into lovely crumbly compost for Janny to put on her flowers, to make them grow strong.

As Lydia approached, the heap burbled and golloped and rippled, and two eyes opened in a head-shaped sort of lump.

"Got anything for old posti?" asked the lump.

"Some yummy potato peelings and crumbly eggshells," said Lydia.

"Ooh, chuck 'em in girly, lovely, nice peelings, crunchy, crunchy, yummy," gurgled the monster happily as Lydia emptied her little pot on to the top of the mound.

While the monster was busy gobbling, Lydia peered in through the murky window of the old woodshed.

"This would make a nice playhouse for me," she said. "I could put all my dollies and teddies inside and make them cups of tea."

Composti Monster almost choked on his eggshells. "Oooh, no missy!" he called. "Not there, not safe. Janny says no!"

Now, Lydia was a bit stubborn and very nosy. "I'll just have a quick look," she said, opening the door, as Composti muttered and shook his lumpy head.

Lydia couldn't see much in the gloom.

She could just make out a few tins of paint, an old watering can, a bucket, some very big cobwebs, a lumpy walking stick and an old-fashioned broom, made out of twigs. Nothing dangerous at all, it seemed. But then the wooden door swung shut behind her with a creak.

"Who have we here then?" said a voice.

"Little girl," said another.

Lydia gulped and looked around but she couldn't see anyone in the shed. Then there was a thumping, bumping sound and the walking stick appeared in front of her! Then there was a shuffling, scratching sound and the broom appeared behind her!

"Who are you?" she whispered.

"I'm Gnarly Broom," said the broom.

"And I'm Thicky Sticky," said the stick, creeping closer. "And we don't like little kiddywinks poking their little noses in, disturbing us."

"Thicky Sticky's just the thing to have when there's a kiddie needs walloping," said the broom, leaning against Lydia's leg.

"Grumps doesn't believe in smacking!" said Lydia, standing her ground.

"That's why I'm banished!" wailed Thicky Sticky. "I used to wallop his bottom lots and lots when he was a little boy, but then he grew up and stuck me down here!"

"I should think so too," said Lydia. "What about Gnarly Broom?"

"Banished too!" cried Thicky Sticky. "Just for being a witch's broom!"

"But Janny's not a witch," said Lydia.

"Course not!" shouted Gnarly Broom. "But Grumps' mummy was – Great Grandma Gwen. Ooh, she was a walloping witch, she was. When she died, all us magicky things got put in this prison. It's not fair!"

"Well, if you go about bashing people and putting nasty spells on them, I'm not surprised," said Lydia, sounding much braver than she felt.

Thicky Sticky edged nearer still. "Talks back a lot, this girly, don't she Gnarly?"

"Nasty, wicked creature," agreed the broom. "Needs a good walloping."

"Wants a good beating," said Thicky and with that, he slammed down on Lydia's toe!

"Ow!" she cried, "That hurt!"

"More where that came from," said the broom and cracked her on the ankle, then bashed her on the knee. "Ow! Get off!" shouted Lydia, but Gnarly clocked her over the back of the head while Thicky Sticky pushed her to the far side of the shed. She was cornered, and as the stick and the broom went thwack! crack! thud! she shouted and shouted for help.

Luckily, Composti Monster heard the commotion and called for Max, who barked for Grumps, who ran down to the end of the garden as fast as he could.

He slammed open the door, striding in to
save his bruised and battered grand-daughter,
who ran out of the shed and hid behind the
compost heap.

"That's it, girly, you're safe with old posti"
said Composti.

Meanwhile Grumps had grasped Thicky
Sticky and hurled him out of the shed. Max
leapt on him at once and chewed him into
a thousand pieces. Then Grumps gripped
Gnarly Broom, who was shrieking and
leaping about, and snapped her in half over
his knee. He got his axe and chopped her up
into a million little pieces. "I should have
done this a long time ago," he said.

Then Lydia swept up all the bits of wood
and threw them to Composti Monster, who
gobbled them up very happily, although he did
complain later that they gave him indigestion.

"Well," said Janny, as she rubbed cream into Lydia's bruises that evening. "Next time maybe you will do as you are told. But I think you've learned your lesson. I guess I'll have to make you some curtains for your new playhouse — I think you've earned it!"

Neptune's Ghost

Old King Neptune sat on his throne, made of beautiful seashells and studded with pearls, and looked around miserably at his underwater castle. It was everything that a royal castle should be, with huge and magnificent rooms, a splendid ballroom, fine chefs in the kitchen and servants to wait on him hand and foot. He even had a court jester.

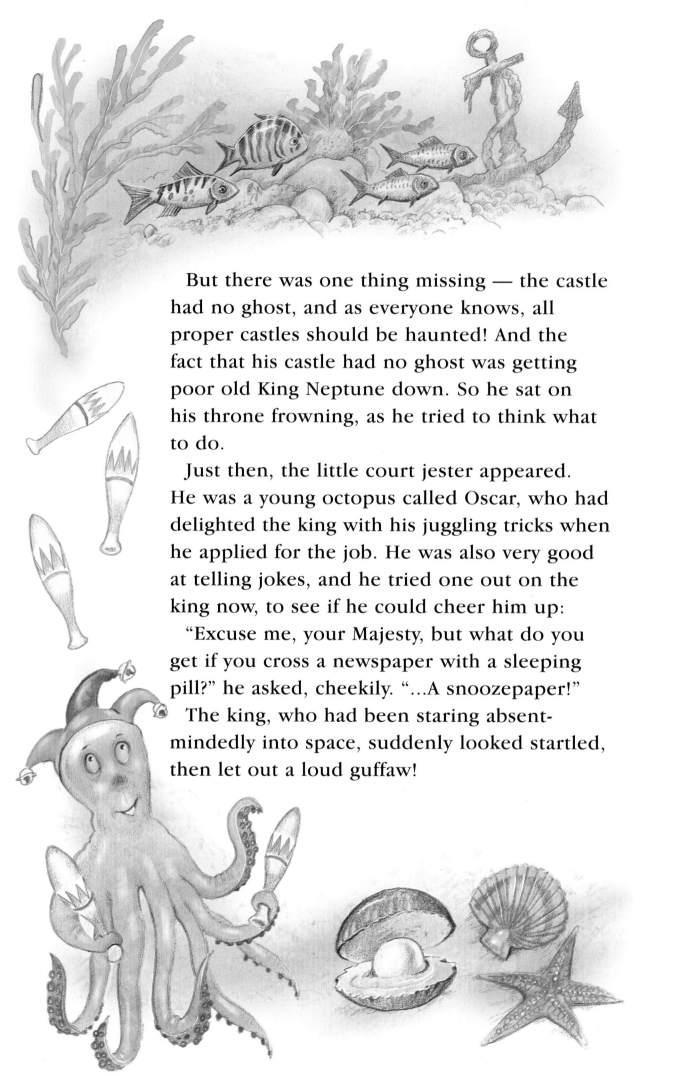

But there was one thing missing — the castle had no ghost, and as everyone knows, all proper castles should be haunted! And the fact that his castle had no ghost was getting poor old King Neptune down. So he sat on his throne frowning, as he tried to think what to do.

Just then, the little court jester appeared. He was a young octopus called Oscar, who had delighted the king with his juggling tricks when he applied for the job. He was also very good at telling jokes, and he tried one out on the king now, to see if he could cheer him up:

"Excuse me, your Majesty, but what do you get if you cross a newspaper with a sleeping pill?" he asked, cheekily. "...A snoozepaper!"

The king, who had been staring absent-mindedly into space, suddenly looked startled, then let out a loud guffaw!

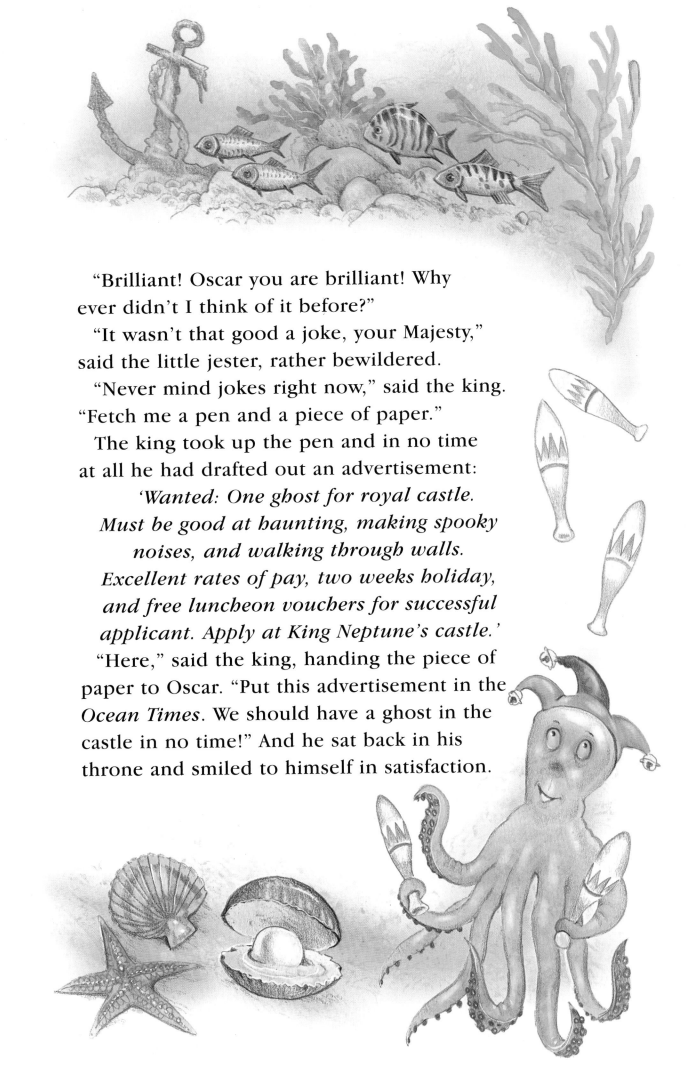

"Brilliant! Oscar you are brilliant! Why ever didn't I think of it before?"

"It wasn't that good a joke, your Majesty," said the little jester, rather bewildered.

"Never mind jokes right now," said the king. "Fetch me a pen and a piece of paper."

The king took up the pen and in no time at all he had drafted out an advertisement:

'Wanted: One ghost for royal castle. Must be good at haunting, making spooky noises, and walking through walls. Excellent rates of pay, two weeks holiday, and free luncheon vouchers for successful applicant. Apply at King Neptune's castle.'

"Here," said the king, handing the piece of paper to Oscar. "Put this advertisement in the *Ocean Times*. We should have a ghost in the castle in no time!" And he sat back in his throne and smiled to himself in satisfaction.

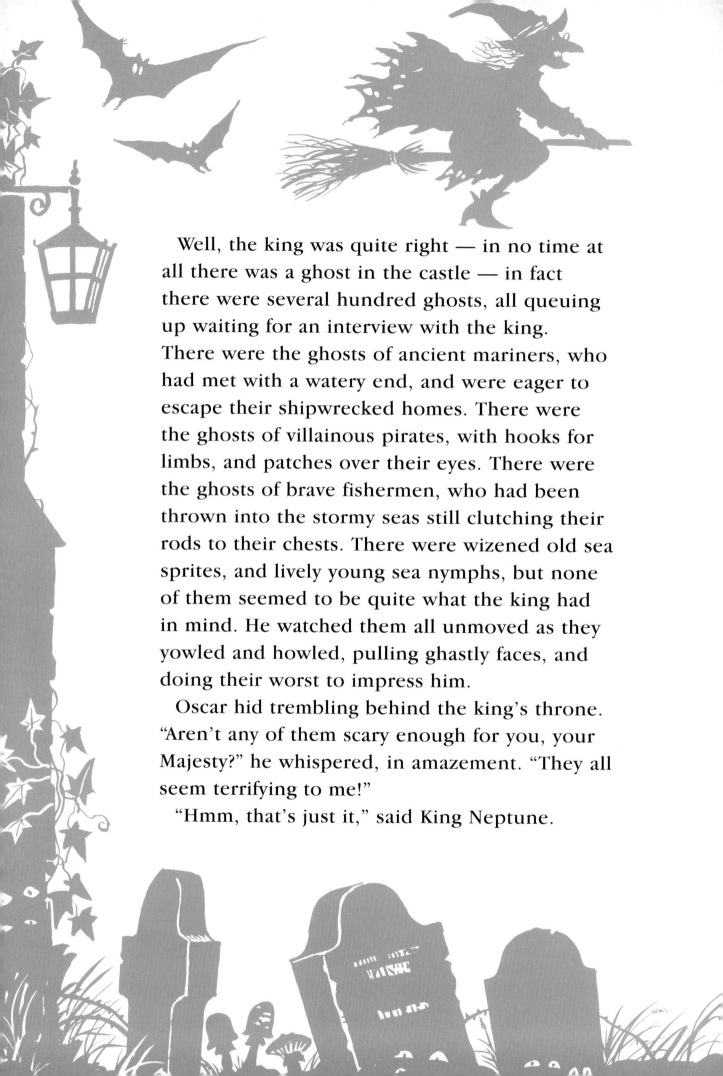

Well, the king was quite right — in no time at
all there was a ghost in the castle — in fact
there were several hundred ghosts, all queuing
up waiting for an interview with the king.
There were the ghosts of ancient mariners, who
had met with a watery end, and were eager to
escape their shipwrecked homes. There were
the ghosts of villainous pirates, with hooks for
limbs, and patches over their eyes. There were
the ghosts of brave fishermen, who had been
thrown into the stormy seas still clutching their
rods to their chests. There were wizened old sea
sprites, and lively young sea nymphs, but none
of them seemed to be quite what the king had
in mind. He watched them all unmoved as they
yowled and howled, pulling ghastly faces, and
doing their worst to impress him.

Oscar hid trembling behind the king's throne.
"Aren't any of them scary enough for you, your
Majesty?" he whispered, in amazement. "They all
seem terrifying to me!"

"Hmm, that's just it," said King Neptune.

"They're all far too scary. Too big, and rough, and ugly. What I really wanted was a little ghost like the one in my storybook." He pulled out a large book from under his throne, and pointed to a picture of a fluffy little white ghost peeking out from behind a fairytale king's throne.

Just then, a haunting little sound echoed in his ears. The king shivered. "What was that?" he asked. But before Oscar could reply, the sound came again, and a fuzzy little white shape came floating through the wall. There before the king hovered the ghost of a little white whale, who had perished when he got caught in some fishing nets, and had been roaming the oceans of the world looking for a home ever since.

The king blinked, and rubbed his eyes.

"Perfect!" he cried and, dismissing all the other applicants, he offered the ghostly little whale the job on the spot. The little whale accepted happily, and the king smiled with satisfaction.

Now his castle had everything that a proper royal castle should have. And so this tale has the ending that every proper fairytale should have — that they all lived happily ever after!

Witches on the Run

At night, when it's all dark and scary,
I peek from my covers, quite wary.
And there on the wall
Are shadows so tall —
Pointed hats, capes and noses all hairy.

My mum says that I must be dreaming,
When I spy witches high on the ceiling.
But they keep me awake
With the noise that they make,
All that ear-piercing cackling and screaming!

They love casting spells late at night,
Their cauldron glows with a strange light.
It bubbles and spits,
Spilling slimy green bits,
And gives me and Teddy a fright!

The things that they use in their spells,
Produce the most terrible smells.
When they toss in a toad
That they've found by the road
You wouldn't believe how it yells!

But tonight when they come I'll be ready,
All I need is to keep my aim steady.
One squirt from my gun,
Will have them on the run,
Witches hate getting wet — don't they Teddy?

They'll jump on their broomsticks and scream,
And wish it was just a bad dream.
They'll fly into the night,
All howling with fright,
Soaked by me and my Ted — what a team!

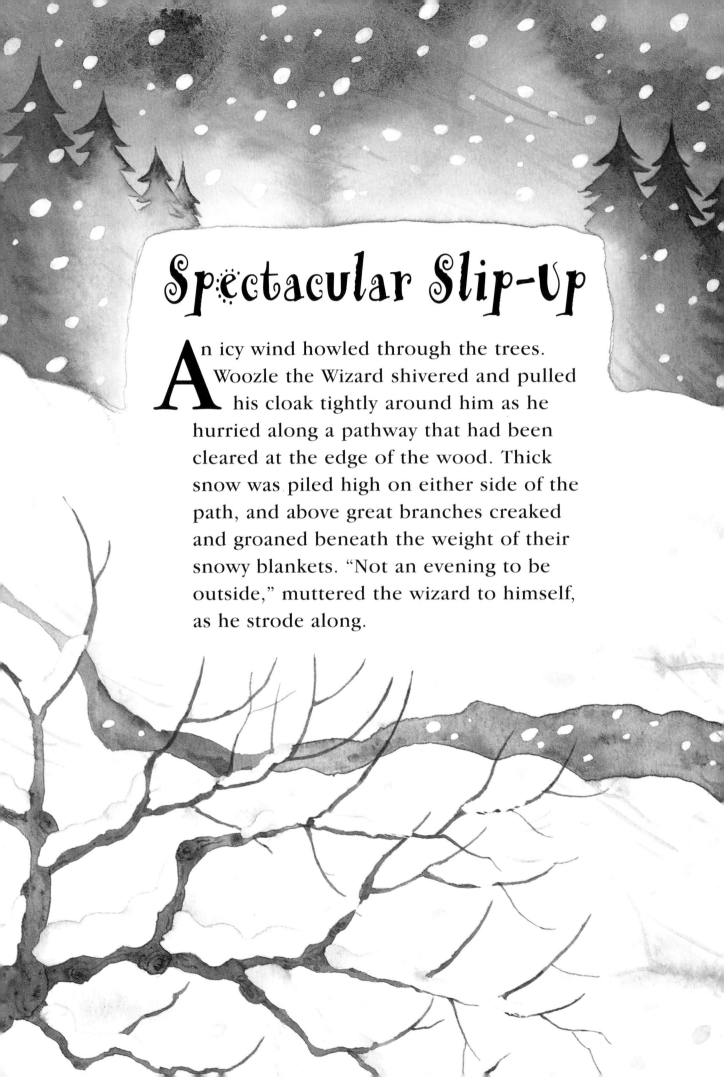

Spectacular Slip-Up

An icy wind howled through the trees. Woozle the Wizard shivered and pulled his cloak tightly around him as he hurried along a pathway that had been cleared at the edge of the wood. Thick snow was piled high on either side of the path, and above great branches creaked and groaned beneath the weight of their snowy blankets. "Not an evening to be outside," muttered the wizard to himself, as he strode along.

But Woozle had no choice. He had promised to deliver an important potion to Mrs Bunny, to cure her babies from an attack of the measles, and he didn't want to let her down.

On his way home, the skies grew even darker, and another snowstorm began. Woozle could barely see the pathway in front of him as he struggled bravely onwards through the storm. Small wonder then, that he didn't see little Mole until it was too late. Mole was scurrying along in the other direction, heading for the warmth of his cosy hole. Then suddenly "Whoomph!", with a crash and a bang, Woozle and Mole collided, sending each other flying! Mole landed upside down in a bank of snow, and Woozle had to pull him out. While Mole felt about in the snow for his glasses, Woozle straightened out the point of his crumpled hat. Then after checking that no-one was hurt, they each continued on their way.

Safe and snug back at home, Woozle settled
down for a nice evening of 'spelling' —
it was time to catch up on some of the new
magic spells he had been waiting to try out.
He took down his spellbook and felt in his
pocket for his reading glasses, but they
weren't there. "Now what have I done with
them?" he muttered to himself crossly.
He looked about but they were nowhere to
be found. "Oh, well, I shall just have to
manage without," he said, and flicked
through the pages of his spellbook. "Ah yes,
here we are — *Spell to Turn Frog into
Teapot*. I could use a new teapot!"

Peering closely at the recipe for the spell,
he gathered the ingredients together and
mixed up a magic potion in his cauldron.
Then, taking a nice fat frog down from the
shelf, he sprinkled it with the potion,
and waved his magic wand.

"Make me a shiny little teapot," cried the wizard. With a crackle and fizz, the frog disappeared and there in its place stood a tiny metal robot.

"Oh, dear," said Woozle. "I must have misread something. Still, a robot could be useful. Go and wait in the corner," he told it, and the little robot did as it was told.

Woozle tried another spell. "This looks simple enough — *Slug into Bowl of Fruit*. Very tasty." But this time when he waved his wand a mug inside a rubber boot appeared. "Well, that's no use at all," sighed Woozle.

He tried to turn a snail into hot buttered toast, but instead he got a fat little ghost, and in place of a chocolate cake he got a garden rake.

"It's no use, I give up," Woozle sighed. He sat back in his favourite armchair and closed his eyes to think. Where had he put his glasses?

Just then he heard a faint scraping at the door.

"Go and open the door," he said to the robot, who happily obliged. Woozle looked out, and there, in a little frozen heap, lay Mole! Woozle leapt to his feet, and helped Mole inside. He wrapped him in a blanket and sat him by the fire.

"Go and make a cup of tea!" he instructed the robot. Soon Woozle and Mole were sipping steaming mugs of tea. "Whatever happened to you, Mole?" asked Woozle.

"I got lost in the snow," said Mole, through chattering teeth. "I've been wandering around in the woods for hours trying to find my way home, but I couldn't see anything clearly because my glasses are broken. Then by a stroke of luck, I came across your door."

Just then, the little ghost popped out from

where he had been hiding behind the sofa. Mole almost dropped his tea in fright, but Woozle shooed the little ghost away. He told Mole about his spells all going wrong.

"I must find my glasses, but I don't know where else to look," said Woozle.

"Why don't you look in your crystal ball?" asked Mole.

"Well, I would, but I need my glasses to see in it clearly," said Woozle.

"Why don't you try mine?" said Mole helpfully. "If we put some tape round the middle, they should be OK!"

Woozle looked doubtful, but he perched them on his nose, and blinked in amazement.

"Perfect!" he said. "They're as good as my own!" He gazed into his crystal ball.

"Can you see anything?" asked Mole, excitedly.

"Yes!", said Woozle, "I can see snow swirling, and someone hurrying along a path. Oh, I can see my glasses lying in the snow! And here I am, bending down to pick them up — no, wait a minute, it's not me, it's you! I can see you, Mole. You're putting the glasses in your pocket!"

"But how can they be mine, when mine are here?" asked Mole, puzzled.

Woozle scratched his head and thought hard.

"I've got it! My glasses must have fallen out of my pocket when we bumped into each other, and you must have picked them up by mistake. Which means that your glasses are still in the snow, and my glasses are, well — they're right here on the end of my nose where they belong!" The two friends chuckled at such a mix-up!

In no time at all, Woozle, using his own
glasses to read the spells carefully this time,
had switched the rubber boot into a bowl
of fruit, and the rake into chocolate cake,
just as he had wanted all along. So, the two
friends tucked into a delicious tea, served up
by the robot, who Woozle decided was more
use than a teapot by far, and entertained by
the little ghost, who Woozle had discovered
was very good at telling spooky stories.

Maybe the long, cold winter would pass
quite pleasantly after all!

Vampire Charms

I woke up this evening, and could not believe
What I saw in my magical mirror.
A face oh so healthy, with rosy red cheeks,
To look at it gave me a shiver.

For I am a vampire and therefore should be
As pale as a glass of cold milk.
With eyes dark as coal, sharp teeth underneath,
And lips like dark ruby red silk.

But oh what has happened here during the day?
I really do not have a notion.
I took all precautions for going to sleep —
Sunglasses and high factor lotion!

But somehow the sunshine has crept through the room,
And entered a chink in my coffin.
To guess what the others will say when they see,
You don't have to be a real boffin!

For they'll laugh and they'll gossip, point fingers and say
"Oh the sunkissed look must be in fashion!
She thinks that a suntan will increase her charm,
When we all know vampires should look ashen!"

So I think I'll stay put in my coffin for now,
At least till this deep tan has faded.
I hope in a while I'll be looking unfit,
And with luck just a little bit jaded!

Peg's Pepper

Think of a witch and the chances are you'll imagine one with a big, black cat, just like Peg and her cat, Pepper. Peg lived in a crooked cottage, deep in a wood. She spent her time making bubbling brews and spectacular spells, which didn't always work. Elves and fairies would ask her to cure anything from a sore tooth to a broken wing. So Peg's time passed busily enough.

She was never lonely either, not with Pepper purring about the place. He followed Peg everywhere. If the witch was in her garden, gathering herbs or other more unpleasant ingredients for the cauldron, Pepper would stalk her through the long grass then pop out playfully. If Peg was sitting by the fire, studying her spell book, then Pepper would curl up contentedly on the witch's lap.

Even when Peg took night flights on her broomstick, Pepper tagged along. He would sink his sharp claws into the handle to get a good grip. Then Peg and Pepper would whizz away up past the moon.

The truth was, Peg and Pepper were perfect company for each other. That is, until something rather strange happened.

"A...atchooo!" Peg suddenly sneezed as she sat gently brushing Pepper's dark fur which shone like polished coal. The witch's long nose began to itch and twitch and her eyes started to water.

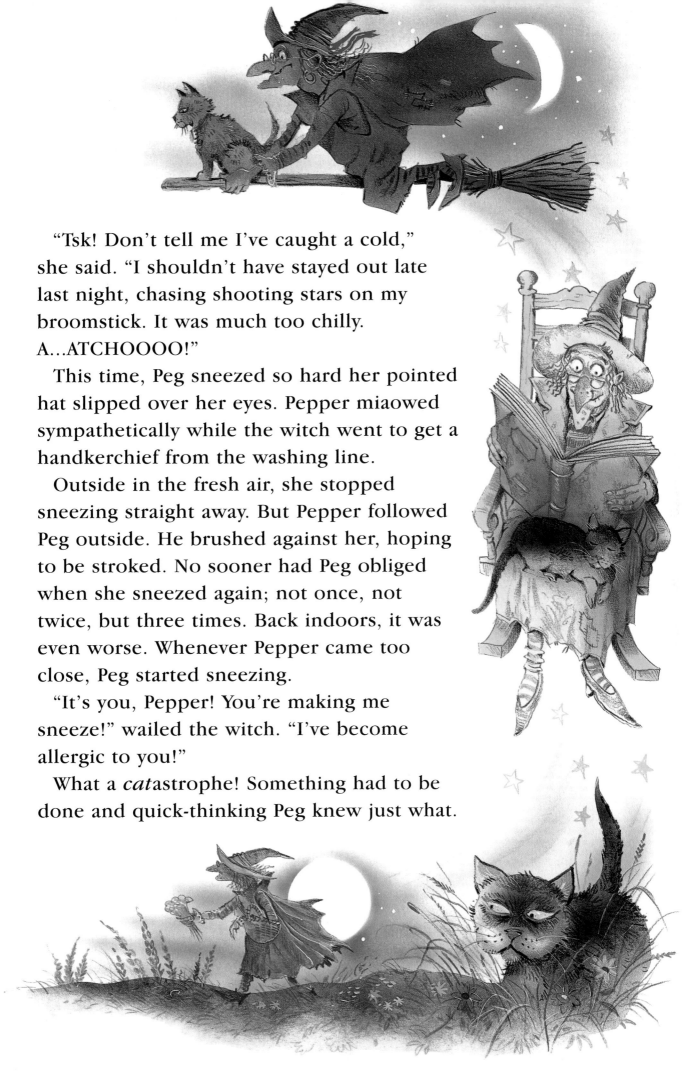

"Tsk! Don't tell me I've caught a cold," she said. "I shouldn't have stayed out late last night, chasing shooting stars on my broomstick. It was much too chilly. A...ATCHOOOO!"

This time, Peg sneezed so hard her pointed hat slipped over her eyes. Pepper miaowed sympathetically while the witch went to get a handkerchief from the washing line.

Outside in the fresh air, she stopped sneezing straight away. But Pepper followed Peg outside. He brushed against her, hoping to be stroked. No sooner had Peg obliged when she sneezed again; not once, not twice, but three times. Back indoors, it was even worse. Whenever Pepper came too close, Peg started sneezing.

"It's you, Pepper! You're making me sneeze!" wailed the witch. "I've become allergic to you!"

What a *cat*astrophe! Something had to be done and quick-thinking Peg knew just what.

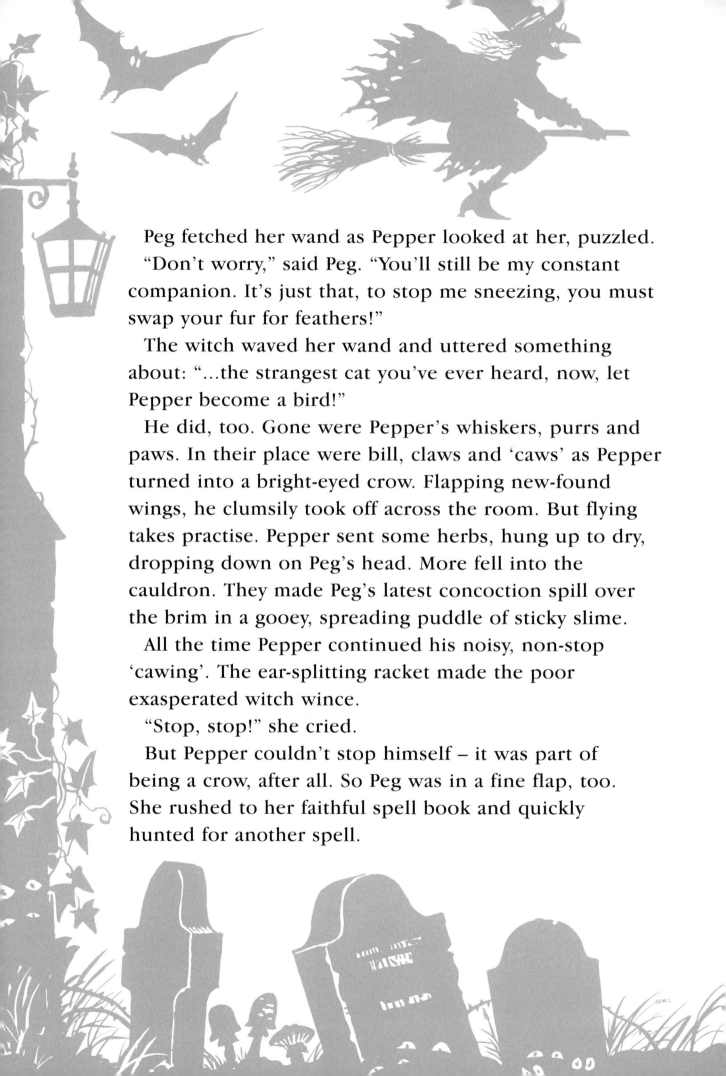

Peg fetched her wand as Pepper looked at her, puzzled.

"Don't worry," said Peg. "You'll still be my constant companion. It's just that, to stop me sneezing, you must swap your fur for feathers!"

The witch waved her wand and uttered something about: "...the strangest cat you've ever heard, now, let Pepper become a bird!"

He did, too. Gone were Pepper's whiskers, purrs and paws. In their place were bill, claws and 'caws' as Pepper turned into a bright-eyed crow. Flapping new-found wings, he clumsily took off across the room. But flying takes practise. Pepper sent some herbs, hung up to dry, dropping down on Peg's head. More fell into the cauldron. They made Peg's latest concoction spill over the brim in a gooey, spreading puddle of sticky slime.

All the time Pepper continued his noisy, non-stop 'cawing'. The ear-splitting racket made the poor exasperated witch wince.

"Stop, stop!" she cried.

But Pepper couldn't stop himself – it was part of being a crow, after all. So Peg was in a fine flap, too. She rushed to her faithful spell book and quickly hunted for another spell.

With a 'POP!', Peg turned Pepper into a toad. He sat, somewhat confused, with big, bulging eyes, on the tabletop. Peg stroked him gently.

"There, there!" she soothed. "I know warty skin isn't a patch on soft, silky fur, Pepper. But at least I've stopped sneezing and you're so much quieter now!"

Pepper hopped unhappily across the flagstone floor then disappeared behind some boxes and bottles. Peg searched everywhere, but Pepper was nowhere to be found.

"He's sulking," thought Peg. "But what else could I do?"

Probably the only place Peg didn't look for Pepper was in her pointed hat, resting on its

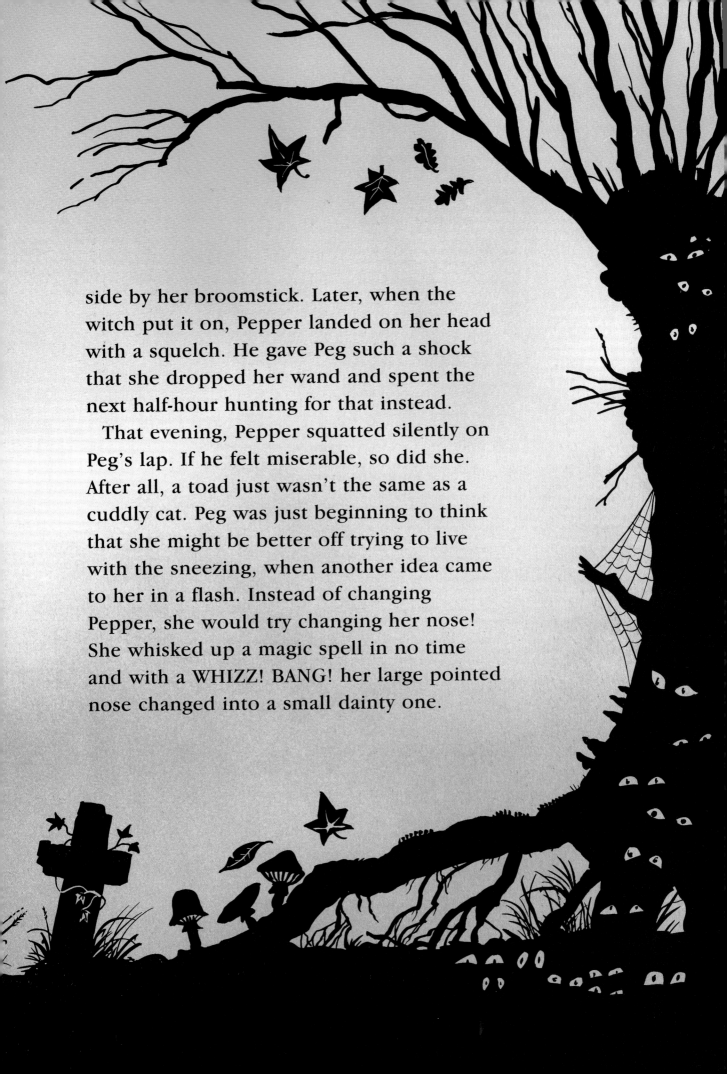

side by her broomstick. Later, when the witch put it on, Pepper landed on her head with a squelch. He gave Peg such a shock that she dropped her wand and spent the next half-hour hunting for that instead.

That evening, Pepper squatted silently on Peg's lap. If he felt miserable, so did she. After all, a toad just wasn't the same as a cuddly cat. Peg was just beginning to think that she might be better off trying to live with the sneezing, when another idea came to her in a flash. Instead of changing Pepper, she would try changing her nose! She whisked up a magic spell in no time and with a WHIZZ! BANG! her large pointed nose changed into a small dainty one.

A further flash from her crooked fingertip spelled goodbye toad and hello cat again. The witch waited eagerly to see if her new nose would solve the problem. Success! Peg didn't sneeze once.

"Magic!" she grinned.

Pepper was delighted to be back to his usual, furry self.

"Not even a tickle from my new, little nose!" cackled Peg, picking up Pepper and stroking him. "I'm cured!"

Pepper purred loudly. But Peg suddenly stopped laughing and uttered a faint sound.

"Hic!"

At the same time, Pepper felt Peg's shoulders shake. It only lasted a moment. But then it happened again, and again.

"Hic! Hic!" The sound only stopped when Peg put Pepper down.

"Great slithering slugs!" shrieked the witch. "My spell's misfired! Now see what you make me do, Pepper!"

But Pepper didn't wait to see anything! He'd had more than his share of changing shape for one day. The last thing he wanted was to be turned into a rat, hedgehog, or anything else Peg may care to think of. Pepper hurtled outside while Peg rushed for her spell book. Thumbing through Magic Cures, she looked up the letter 'H'.

"'Hairy hands, horrible howls'," she read, urgently. "I know it's here somewhere. How *do* you spell hiccups?!"

The Hungry Ghost

Becky had just sat down to have breakfast (scrambled eggs and bacon), when something very strange happened. The salt and pepper pots rose up from the table and floated through the air towards her father's plate, where his breakfast sat waiting for him to appear. Becky's jaw dropped open in surprise.

"Mum!" she called to her mother.
"The pepper pot's floating in mid-air!"

"Very nice, darling," called her mum, who
was watching breakfast television and not
paying attention.

Becky looked back at the table. There, in her
father's chair, sat a little ghost with a napkin
around his neck, holding a knife and fork.
He was tucking into her father's breakfast.

"Very good!" said the ghost. "Bacon's a bit
salty, mind you!"

Becky could not believe her eyes!

"Mum!" she shouted. "Look! There's a ghost
eating Daddy's breakfast!"

"What's that? More toast for breakfast?"
called her mum, distractedly. "Just coming!"

The hungry little ghost gobbled his way
through the scrambled eggs and three slices

of toast. He drank a glass of orange juice and two cups of coffee. Then he let out an enormous burp.

"Pardon me!" he said to Becky.

Becky sat open-mouthed and did not dare to answer him. Just then her father hurried into the room, tucking his shirt into his trousers and fiddling with his tie.

"Good morning, Becky," he said, kissing her on the top of her head. He looked over at his place at the table and scowled at his empty plate.

"Where's my breakfast?" he demanded. "Surely you haven't eaten it, Becky?"

Becky looked over at where the little ghost had been sitting. He was gone.

"It wasn't me, Dad, it was the ghost!" Becky answered quickly. "Honest!"

"Ghost? Don't be ridiculous, there are no such things as ghosts!" said her dad, impatiently.

"But there was, Dad. He was sitting right there in your chair. He even used your napkin!" Becky protested, pointing to the screwed-up napkin.

"Becky, I don't have time for this nonsense. I'm late for work!" said her father, crossly. "Sandra, where's my breakfast gone?" he called to his wife. Becky's mum came in, and blinked in astonishment when she saw the empty plate.

"I put it right there," she said in amazement. "Becky can't have eaten yours *and* hers!"

"I didn't," Becky protested. "It was the ghost!"

"Oh, really, Becky! I've had enough of this. Go to your room!" snapped her father.

Becky stood up to do as she was told. But as she did so, she caught sight of the armchair and smiled. "Well, if you don't believe me, look behind you," she said.

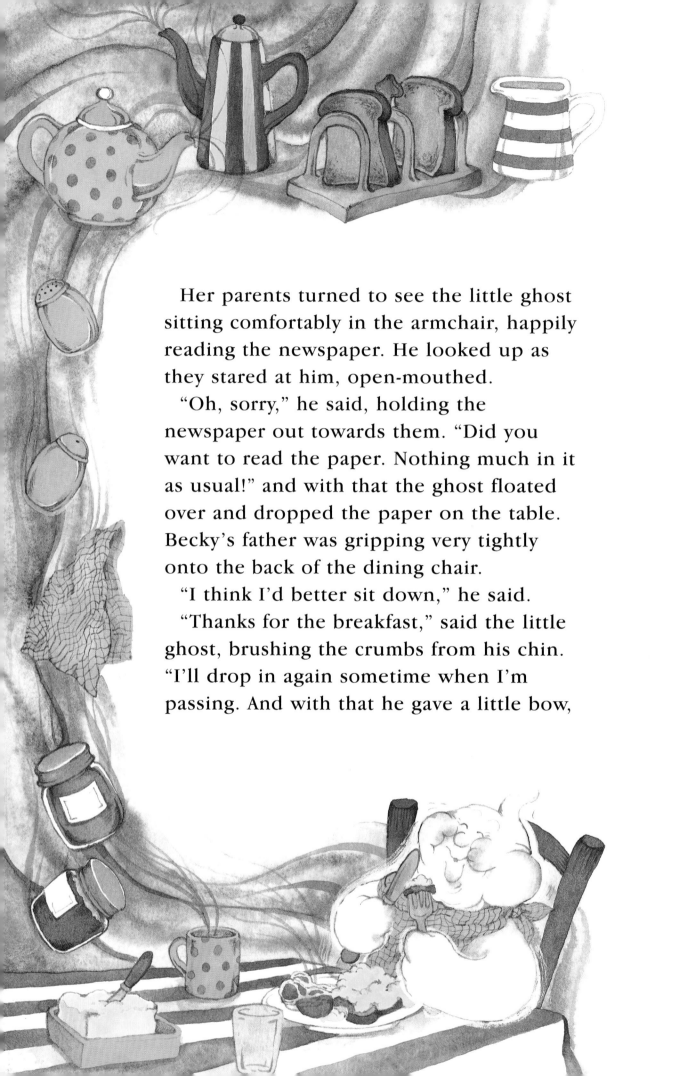

Her parents turned to see the little ghost sitting comfortably in the armchair, happily reading the newspaper. He looked up as they stared at him, open-mouthed.

"Oh, sorry," he said, holding the newspaper out towards them. "Did you want to read the paper. Nothing much in it as usual!" and with that the ghost floated over and dropped the paper on the table. Becky's father was gripping very tightly onto the back of the dining chair.

"I think I'd better sit down," he said.

"Thanks for the breakfast," said the little ghost, brushing the crumbs from his chin. "I'll drop in again sometime when I'm passing. And with that he gave a little bow,

and disappeared through the wall.

Becky's dad blinked and rubbed his eyes. He looked at his wife, who simply spread out her hands and shrugged her shoulders. Then he looked at Becky, who was smiling triumphantly.

"I told you," she said. Finally, he looked down at the table and sat staring at the paper in stunned silence.

"I don't believe it!" he said at last, amazed. "He's even finished the crossword!"

A Jittery Journey

The moon's like a wizard's face up in the sky,
The night is as black as a cat.
The trees branches rustle and wave as you pass,
Then reach down to snatch off your hat.

The wind wants to whisper a secret to you,
An owl hoots, "Nooo! Nooo! Mustn't tell!"
You can hear a dog howling (or is it a wolf?),
And the chimes of a distant church bell.

A monster is lying in wait by the path —
With hundreds of feet and big teeth!
Or is it a tree fallen, struck in a storm,
With toadstools now growing beneath?

Quick! Is that a light you can see through the wood.
Hurry up, there are bats flying round!
Here you are at the gate — Mum opens the door,
And you're home once again — safe and sound!

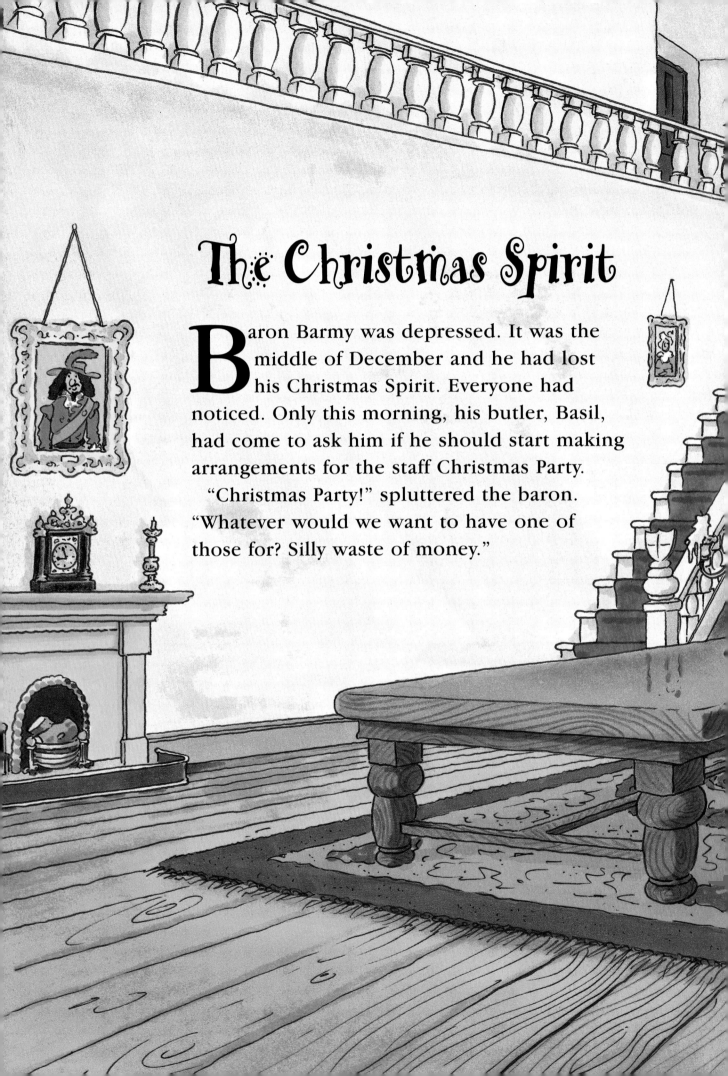

The Christmas Spirit

Baron Barmy was depressed. It was the middle of December and he had lost his Christmas Spirit. Everyone had noticed. Only this morning, his butler, Basil, had come to ask him if he should start making arrangements for the staff Christmas Party.

"Christmas Party!" spluttered the baron. "Whatever would we want to have one of those for? Silly waste of money."

"But with all due respect, sir, we have one every year," said Basil, baffled. "Where's your Christmas Spirit?"

"I don't know," said the baron. "And what is more, I don't care. You can tell the staff that this year Christmas is cancelled. It will be business as usual."

"Cancelled!" said Basil in amazement. "What do you mean, cancelled?"

"No decorations, no Christmas dinner, no time off and definitely no parties," said the baron. "Cancelled. Is that understood?"

"But you *love* Christmas, sir," protested Basil. "It's always been your favourite time of year."

"Well, not this year," said Baron Barmy with a sniff, and he stomped out of the room, muttering crossly to himself.

He was sitting at the breakfast table, trying to concentrate on the crossword, when the Head Chef came to see him.

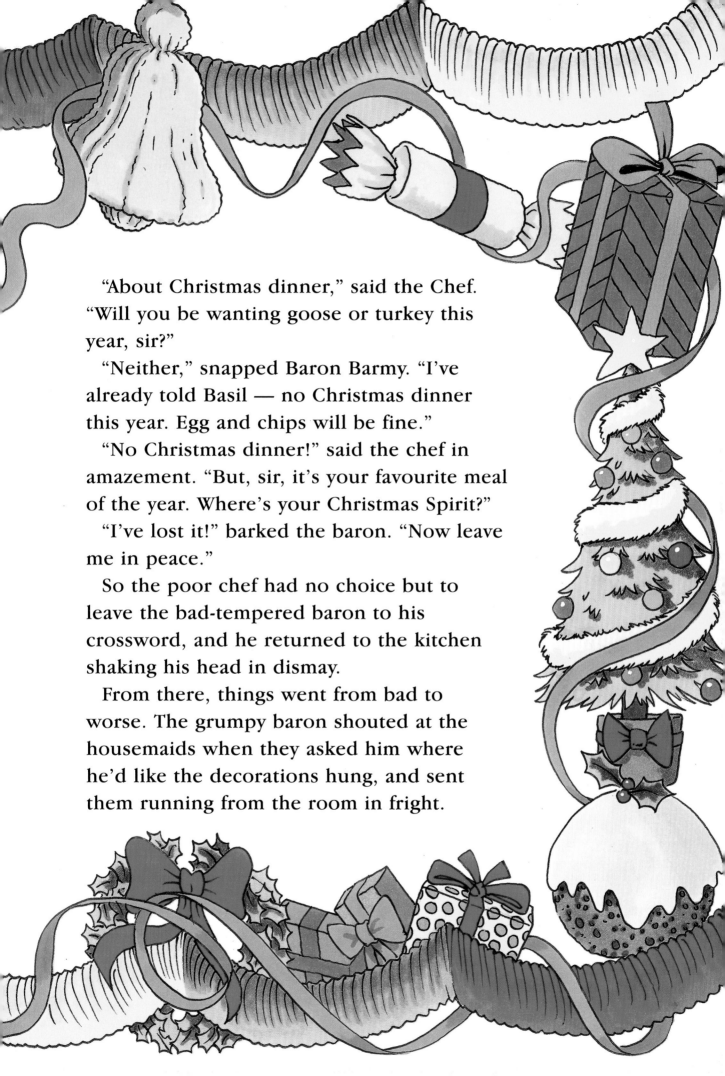

"About Christmas dinner," said the Chef. "Will you be wanting goose or turkey this year, sir?"

"Neither," snapped Baron Barmy. "I've already told Basil — no Christmas dinner this year. Egg and chips will be fine."

"No Christmas dinner!" said the chef in amazement. "But, sir, it's your favourite meal of the year. Where's your Christmas Spirit?"

"I've lost it!" barked the baron. "Now leave me in peace."

So the poor chef had no choice but to leave the bad-tempered baron to his crossword, and he returned to the kitchen shaking his head in dismay.

From there, things went from bad to worse. The grumpy baron shouted at the housemaids when they asked him where he'd like the decorations hung, and sent them running from the room in fright.

He stamped and shook his fists when a delivery man tried to deliver a ten-foot Christmas tree for the Baronial Hall, and sent him, trembling, on his way. He tore up every Christmas card he received, and threw a bucket of cold water from an upstairs window onto some poor unsuspecting carol singers. Then he stomped up to his bedroom and went to bed, hanging a large *Do Not Disturb* sign on his door.

Now you may be thinking that Baron Barmy sounds like a very mean and nasty baron indeed. But the truth is that the baron was really very miserable. He had always loved Christmas, and would have liked nothing more than a huge celebration.

But this year, although he had hunted high and low, he could not find his Christmas Spirit anywhere, and he simply could not imagine celebrating Christmas without it. He pulled the bedcovers up to his chin, and frowned as he concentrated and thought as hard as he could. "Where, oh, where did I put it? It must be somewhere safe..."

All night long he sat up thinking, but still the answer would not come. Then, as he lay dozing, the first streaks of early morning sunshine spilled in through his window and he woke with a start.

"I've got it!" he cried, and he leapt from his bed in a flash, and ran across the room to a huge chest of drawers standing in the corner.

He rummaged through his sock drawer, throwing all manner of socks and underpants around the room in his excitement, until there, at the very bottom of the huge drawer he spied a tiny red box. He took off the lid, and with a whoosh and a bright sweep of twinkling stars, a little ghost in a red santa hat appeared.

"Oh, thank goodness!" sighed the baron. "I thought I'd lost you!"

The little Christmas Spirit had been in the baron's family for years, handed down from generation to generation as a magical secret heirloom. Just one glimpse of the jolly little ghost was enough to fill the kind old baron's heart full of Christmas cheer. Now the little ghost would help him plan a wonderful Christmas to remember!

"You have no idea how terrible it has been to think of having Christmas without you," said the baron to his little friend. "Come along, we've got lots of work to do."

And with the little ghost floating happily at his side, he ran out into the corridor, and down the great marble staircase, still wearing his nightshirt.

"I've found it! I've found it everyone! I've found my Christmas Spirit!" he cried.

Gathering his bemused staff together in the Great Hall, Baron Barmy called for silence as he made a grand announcement:

"Ladies and gentlemen, it is my great pleasure to inform you that this is going to be the best Christmas that has ever been celebrated in this Hall!"

In no time at all he had organised a wonderful Christmas celebration, with music and lights and beautiful decorations. A huge tree was placed in the Baronial Hall, there were presents for everyone, and the staff had the most marvellous Christmas party ever.

Of course, they all thought the baron was barmy, as no one else could see the little ghost but him. But then they had always thought he was nutty — nutty but awfully

nice. And of course, they were just glad that Christmas was back on again.

And so, as the baron carved an extra slice of turkey for the little ghosts' plate at the Christmas dinner table, Basil the butler was more than happy to raise a toast:

"To the Christmas Spirit," he said.

"The Christmas Spirit," echoed all the staff, and they tucked into their dinner.

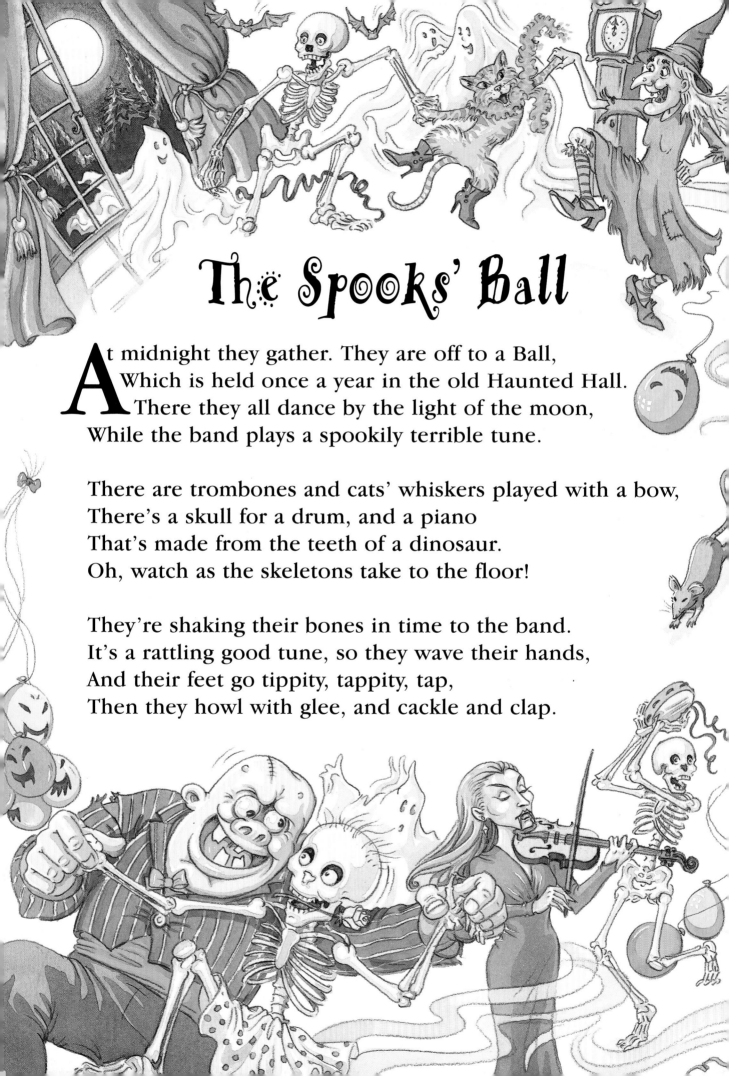

The Spooks' Ball

At midnight they gather. They are off to a Ball,
Which is held once a year in the old Haunted Hall.
There they all dance by the light of the moon,
While the band plays a spookily terrible tune.

There are trombones and cats' whiskers played with a bow,
There's a skull for a drum, and a piano
That's made from the teeth of a dinosaur.
Oh, watch as the skeletons take to the floor!

They're shaking their bones in time to the band.
It's a rattling good tune, so they wave their hands,
And their feet go tippity, tappity, tap,
Then they howl with glee, and cackle and clap.

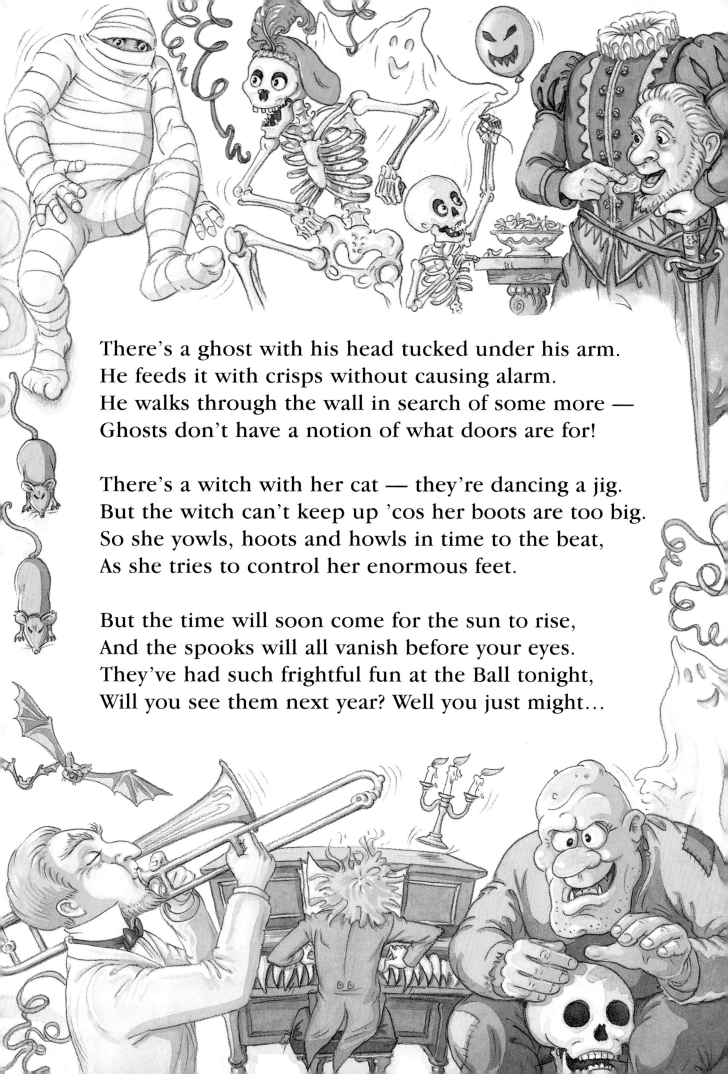

There's a ghost with his head tucked under his arm.
He feeds it with crisps without causing alarm.
He walks through the wall in search of some more —
Ghosts don't have a notion of what doors are for!

There's a witch with her cat — they're dancing a jig.
But the witch can't keep up 'cos her boots are too big.
So she yowls, hoots and howls in time to the beat,
As she tries to control her enormous feet.

But the time will soon come for the sun to rise,
And the spooks will all vanish before your eyes.
They've had such frightful fun at the Ball tonight,
Will you see them next year? Well you just might…